Christmas at Edgewood Park

Christmas at Edgewood Park

SHAELA KAY

Blue Water Books

Other books in this series

Christmas at Cartwright Manor

Published by Blue Water Books
Richland, WA

Cover photo © Adobe Stock/fotorince

© 2017 Shaela Kay Odd
Visit the author at www.shaelakay.com

This book is a work of fiction. While great care has been taken to ensure historical accuracy of dates and locations, characters and events in this book are products of the author's imagination and are represented fictitiously. Any likeness to any person, living or dead, is purely coincidental.

For Carrie, Erin, and Sachiko.
Thanks for being awesome.

Chapter 1

October 1841
Littleton, Norfolk, England

Mr. Franklin Cartwright had been dead for a fortnight, but the neighborhood in which his estate lay did not miss him in the least. On the contrary, the townspeople of Littleton rather rejoiced at his passing, for he had been a sour, miserly man, whose only comfort seemed to be in criticizing his neighbors and gloating over his wealth. His son and heir, Albert Cartwright, had not been seen in the country for many years, and did not return for his father's funeral. In fact, the only ones in attendance at the grave event were the minister and his wife, his neighbor Mr. Eves, and Mr. Eves's daughter, Eleanor.

Eleanor Eves was a pretty young woman, though perhaps *young* would not be the best description of her. She was nearing thirty, and by all accounts was an old maid. Her fortune, though modest, had never been grand enough to tempt any man of particular wealth or position, and having spent only one season in London, she had never received an offer of marriage. This, however, did not bother Eleanor very much. She enjoyed her independence, relished her position, and delighted in running the household of her aging father.

Having lost the bloom but not the vigor of her youth, her life was as busy and cheerful as she could wish for. Her position in society left her time and means to be of service to many of her neighbors, and for several years her pet project had been organizing an annual holiday bazaar, to benefit the less fortunate members of the parish.

It was late in October when our story opens, and Eleanor was visiting the home of Mrs. Lewis, the minister's wife.

"I hope to secure all the usual donations," she said. "Mrs. Matheson has agreed to make some of her delicious pies, Mrs. Sotherby is donating a quilt, and Miss Anderson has several jars of plum preserves to contribute."

"I am nearly finished knitting a new shawl," her friend replied. "You are welcome to have that as well."

"Oh, thank you! Your knitting is so fine, I am sure it will fetch a handsome price."

The ladies were having tea together, as they often did. Though the minister and his wife were closer in age to her father than herself, Eleanor found Mrs. Lewis's company so agreeable, that the two had become very close friends.

"When is the bazaar to be?"

"The week before Christmas, as usual. Father Lewis has

already given his permission to use the chapel again this year."

Mrs. Lewis chuckled. "I remember how appalled he was, when we first came to the neighborhood, to hear what you had planned. You brazenly declared that the previous minister had always allowed you to move the pews out of the way and set up shop in the church, and you expected him to do the same."

Eleanor laughed. "Oh, dear me, yes! How impertinent I was! But it really is the best place for it. Edgewood is so far out of the way for most people, and the chapel so large and convenient, that it does not make sense to hold it anywhere else. I hope he has forgiven me."

Her friend smiled. "Indeed he has. Your care and concern for the less fortunate has endeared you to him in such a way, that I believe you could propose turning the chapel into a circus and he would agree wholeheartedly."

The ladies enjoyed their afternoon together, and at the end of it, Eleanor took her leave. The Lewises lived in a small apartment attached to the church, at the end of the main road in the village. This meant that Eleanor had to travel a few miles to the south of town to reach her own home at Edgewood Park. The road thither passed over a narrow river and through a beautiful grove of trees. Ash, chestnut, and oak grew together in abundance, but only a few shriveled leaves clung tenaciously to their branches. Eleanor watched through the window of the carriage as the trees flashed past, wondering when they would be covered in snow.

She soon turned down the long, tree-lined lane leading to Edgewood Park. Having spent nearly her entire life in Norfolk, the modest home was very dear to her. It had nearly two dozen rooms, and was the largest in the neighborhood next to

3

Cartwright Manor, which lay two miles to the west. Sprawling lawns and cozy little copses dotted the park, which was far more grand than the house situated on it. But Eleanor did not mind. There was no place on earth she would rather be than at Edgewood Park.

The horses pulled up to the main entrance and Eleanor alighted from the carriage, climbing the steps to the front door. "Is my father at home?" she asked a footman upon entering the house.

"Yes, miss. He is in the library."

"Thank you, James." She removed her bonnet and gloves, handing them to him, then made her way down the hall. She paused when she heard voices coming from the study.

It appeared that Mr. Eves had a guest.

Knocking lightly on the door, she was bid to enter by her father. "Papa?" she called, stepping into the room. "I heard voices, are you—Nathan!"

Grinning, a young man with ginger curls and laughing eyes stood, and Eleanor ran to embrace her younger brother. "Oh, Nathaniel! How glad I am that you are home! When did you arrive?"

"Not a half hour ago."

"I am sorry I was not here to greet you."

"Oh, never mind that. Father and I have been catching up on things between us. How are you?"

"Very well, thank you," Eleanor said, releasing her brother and taking a seat beside him on the sofa. "I am beginning my preparations for the holiday bazaar."

"That is not all you are beginning, from what I understand," her brother said. "Father said you are having the drawing room redone?"

Eleanor beamed. "Yes, indeed! He has at last given his permission, and I have had a marvelous time selecting draperies and carpet and all new furnishings."

"And cleaning out my pocketbook in the process," Mr. Eves interjected.

Laughing, Eleanor shook her finger at her father. "You shall not make me feel guilty, sir, for I have been staying well within the budget you gave me, Papa. You said yourself it was deplorable how threadbare the carpet and furniture had become."

"Indeed I did, my dear," Mr. Eves said, chuckling. "And the choices you have made will make a lovely addition to our home."

She gave him an affectionate smile, and turned back to her brother. "How are things at Cambridge?"

Nathaniel sighed. "Tediously dull, I'm afraid. I'm looking forward to some fun and frolic now that I am home." He winked at her, and she laughed.

"Here, in Littleton? I cannot imagine what sort of mischief you can get into here that you could not have got into at school."

"Perhaps Nathaniel plans to upset your little bazaar," her father added helpfully.

Eleanor scoffed. "He certainly shall not, or he shall answer to *me.*"

The afternoon and evening passed most pleasantly. The Eves talked of colleges, news, and neighbors—the only real objects which governed their little world. When at last the day was spent and they had bid goodnight to their father, Eleanor and Nathaniel spent a few quiet moments together.

"Are you happy here, Nora?" her brother asked, when they were at last alone.

"Of course," she replied, surprised. "Why do you ask?"

He shrugged. "I worry about you, taking care of Father, and the house, all by yourself. I know you feel it your duty, and that you are happy to help, but, well..." He hesitated. "You only had one season in London, Nora."

"Nathan," Eleanor said, gently but firmly. "You know perfectly well how much I detest town life. London is so crowded I could hardly breathe! No, I would much prefer to live out my days in the country. I love our home, and am happy to care for our father in it."

"I know," he said quickly. "But Nora, if you went to town for another season, perhaps..." He pulled on his cravat, avoiding her gaze. "Perhaps you might meet with a gentleman whose company you enjoy. You could settle down in a house of your own, and have a family," he finished in a rush.

"Go to town!" she cried, laughing. "Heaven forbid!" But her look softened, and she laid a hand on his arm. "Nathan, I thank you for your concern. But do you suppose that any man would so much as look at me, at my age in life? Perhaps if I were a wealthy heiress, or if Father were titled... but no," she said, more firmly than before. "I am far happier with my lot in life than any other I might choose at present."

Her brother sighed. "I can see your point. But if you ever desire to have another season, or wish to travel abroad... you know our father has given me a handsome allowance. I would be a sorry brother indeed if I spent it all on myself. Which reminds me," he said, pulling a small, paper-wrapped parcel from his pocket. "This is for you."

"Dear Nathaniel! You know the only gift I desire is more time with you at home."

He shrugged. "I saw them in a shop window and thought of you."

Eleanor carefully unwrapped the stiff paper, revealing a beautiful pair of gloves. They were finely woven silk, dyed a lovely shade of gray. Two pearl buttons adorned each glove at the wrist, and Eleanor picked them up with a soft *oh!*

"Nathan, they are beautiful!" She slipped them on, fastening the buttons and holding her hands out to admire them. Her brother smiled.

"I'm glad you like them. I daresay you have a dozen pairs already, but as I said before, I saw them in the shop and felt you must have them."

"They are perfectly lovely, and I feel quite spoilt, for you always bring me gifts when you come home. Whatever shall I do when you get married?"

"Married!" Nathaniel laughed.

"But of course! You are sure to meet a pretty young lady one of these days, who will whisk your heart away and take you away with it."

"And where, pray tell, would we go?"

"Oh, wherever it is young lovers run off to these days. I hear Bath is very pleasant," she teased.

"If you are so determined to be rid of me, I shall find the first eligible lady of my acquaintance and happily oblige."

"As long as she is prettier than I am, mind. I could not abide a jealous sister."

Nathaniel rolled his eyes. "Be serious, Nora. How can you believe I would run off and leave you and our father?"

She laid her head on his shoulder. "I was only teasing you, Nathan. I know you care for me far more deeply than I probably deserve."

His look softened. "You underrate yourself, Nora."

"Perhaps," she said, rising from her place. "But I know that you will always be here to make me feel better about myself."

She bid him goodnight and retired to her room. Long after the lamps were out and she had crawled beneath the covers, she pondered the question her brother had posed. She had spoken the truth in her reply—she *was* happy to be helping their father and running his household. But despite the assurances to her brother, Eleanor could not deny that deep in heart she longed for a home, and a family, of her own.

Chapter 2

Albert pulled his horse to a stop and surveyed the building before him, his dislike growing the longer he looked upon it. His childhood home held nothing but bitter memories for him, and had it been in his power, he would have sold it the moment it fell into his possession. But though it belonged to him by right of primogeniture, the details of the entail made it impossible for him to part with any portion of it, so as to *"preserve the estate in its entirety for the benefit of your firstborn son."* That is what Franklin Cartwright's will had stated.

His face twisted into a sneer at the thought. When had any woman looked on him with anything but horror? Did his father honestly believe the time would come when he would not be rejected and despised by society?

His horse stamped its feet in the chilly air, blowing clouds of steam from his nostrils. Albert bent down and patted his neck, then swung himself out of the saddle. He grunted as his foot hit the ground, sending a jolt of familiar pain up his leg. Reaching up, he pulled his walking stick from its leather sheath. He had had the saddle custom-made in London, to accommodate the cane he always carried with him. Refastening the buckles, he took the reins in his right hand and leaned upon the cane in his left, leading his mount towards the stables.

The chill in the air made his muscles stiff, accentuating his limp. Despite his crooked gait, Albert was sure in his steps—the lapse of three-and-twenty years since the accident having engendered him with confidence, if not improvement, while walking.

Guiding his horse around the manor, he looked up at the moss-covered stones stretching three stories above his head. He had not spent more than a fortnight within those walls in almost a decade, and he did not intend to make this return a permanent one. Though he had not received the news of his father's death in time to return for the funeral service, Albert knew he would be required to meet with both his steward and his barrister, now that the property had fallen to him.

As he was turning the corner around the house, he was spotted by a groomsman, who came running from the stables.

"Master Cartwright! Welcome home... sir."

The young man quickly averted his gaze. Albert did not recognize him, but judging from both his greeting and his reaction, his master's appearance was not wholly unexpected. Albert handed the reins to the man and turned away.

"Please see that my horse is fed and groomed. I shall not be needing him until morning."

"Yes, sir."

Albert walked back towards the house, dread filling his heart. How many other new servants would he be forced to meet before at last finding solace in his chambers? The young groomsman had obviously been informed of the disfiguration of his new master—the look of abhorrence on his face had certainly betrayed *that.* And though Albert was accustomed to the stares and whispers that followed him in public, he had usually been safe from them at home.

Home. Albert laughed humorlessly to himself. Cartwright Manor was more a tomb than a home.

A set of round stone steps led up from the lawn to the back entrance, and Albert climbed them without pausing. Opening the door, he stepped inside the house, memories swirling in his mind like a heavy fog.

"Merciful heavens!" a woman shrieked. Albert turned in her direction.

"Hello, Mrs. Winthrop."

"Master Albert," the woman said, clutching at her chest. "What a fright you gave me! Why did you not come in the front entrance? We have been watching for your arrival since Tuesday."

"There is a new groomsman," Albert said, ignoring her question. "Who else is new to the household?"

"You must be referring to Crenshaw's nephew," the housekeeper said, bending to pick up the pile of linens she had dropped. "He came on the summer before last. We have a few new housemaids as well, but they have all been informed that if they so much as mention your ailments, they shall be dismissed forthwith."

Albert turned away, irritated. He did not wish to be treated as if he had the plague. Of course, he did not want to be gawked at and gossiped over, either, but even that was better than being pitied. He hated their pity.

Knowing the old housekeeper meant well, he pulled his lips into a one-sided smile and thanked her.

He limped his way into the drawing room, thankful to find a comfortable fire waiting for him. At first glance, the room seemed very much as it ever had been. A massive rock fireplace, nearly eight feet wide, dominated the space. Ancient tapestries and worn velvet carpets hid the cold stone of the floors and walls as best they could, but the gloom which permeated the house was not something that could be easily concealed.

Sitting down in front of the fire, Albert shut his eyes against the room around him. It was too familiar, too painful. He thought to himself that he would have it refurnished as soon as possible, until he remembered that he did not plan to stay, and would be gone again soon.

The thought was like a breath of fresh air.

Though well-provided for, his childhood had not been a happy one. Albert's scars had always served as a bitter reminder of the horrific accident which had claimed his mother's life, and left him a cripple. He had always wondered if his father had treated him so harshly because Franklin Cartwright had wished that it had been *Albert's* life that had been lost, and his mother's spared. Whether it was true or not, there was no question that Franklin Cartwright had never been the same after the accident. All affection seemed to have died with Marguerite, and towards his only son he became somewhat of a monster. Critical and controlling, he was the only one in the household who dared to draw attention to the scars which disfigured his son's face, and Albert hated him for it.

A knock at the door pulled Albert out of his reverie, and he gladly turned his attention elsewhere. It was his housekeeper again, coming in with a tray of food.

"I expect you're famished, Master Albert, after such a long journey."

"Yes."

"Where were you when you heard of your father's passing?"

"At Vienna."

She shook her head, marveling. "You've seen so much of the world, for such a young man."

He gave no answer.

"Tilda will be bringing in your tea. Have you need of anything else?"

"Please see to it that the bed in my old chambers is turned and ready. I shall be retiring as soon as I have eaten."

"Yes, sir."

His housekeeper curtsied and left the room, leaving Albert alone once more.

Chapter 3

"Mistress, have you heard the news?"

Eleanor looked up from the letter she was writing. Her housekeeper bobbed a curtsy and continued excitedly, without waiting for an answer. "Albert Cartwright has returned to the manor!"

Eleanor's jaw dropped open. "Albert Cartwright?"

"Yes, miss."

She frowned. "Are you sure?"

"Yes, miss. Ruthie Harrison works in the kitchens there, and she told her mother that he arrived last night."

"He was not even here for his father's funeral," Eleanor said, more to herself than her housekeeper. She was then silent, and after a few moments her servant spoke again.

"Just thought you'd like to know, miss. Seeing as how we're such close neighbors."

"Yes," Eleanor said, distracted. "Thank you, Mrs. Fielding." Picking up her quill once more, she added, "Will you please see to it that the library has a large enough fire? I do not want my father to take chill."

"Of course, miss."

The housekeeper curtsied again and left the room. When she had gone, Eleanor laid down her pen, all thought of the letter she was writing having fled her mind.

Albert Cartwright was home.

The news was more than surprising—it was wholly and completely unexpected. The man had not set foot in Littleton for years, and when he *had* been a resident, he, like his father, had mostly kept to himself. He was a strange man, and nobody really knew anything about him, other than the fact that he was horribly disfigured. Most of the town knew it was the result of a carriage accident in his youth, but a few whispered that old Mr. Cartwright had maimed his son himself. Eleanor, however, did not believe that for a moment. Even as ill-tempered and ornery as Franklin Cartwright had been, she could not believe him capable of such cruelty.

Not long after Eleanor herself had received the information of Mr. Cartwright's arrival, the entire neighborhood was buzzing with the news.

"He's back—Albert Cartwright is back!"

"Have you seen him?"

"Where do you think he's been all these years?"

"Land sakes, I never thought I'd see the day!"

" 'Bout time he turned up, I say."

"I wonder when we'll see him?"

There was a great deal of gossip concerning his unexpected arrival, but as no one had actually seen him yet or spoken with the man, not very much was known of the matter. Most people assumed he was there only to conduct the business left to him since the death of his father, or at the very most, to hunt for a few weeks and be gone again by Christmas. The son, shrouded in mystery, had been absent so long, and the general prejudice against his father was so severe, that no one looked on his return with a friendly eye.

Mrs. Lewis came to call a few days after the news had circulated. "What is all this I hear about Albert Cartwright? I barely even knew of his existence before, but he is all anyone can talk of now."

"Albert Cartwright is the estranged son of the late Mr. Franklin Cartwright. He left the country many years ago, and has not been seen or heard from since."

"And is he a hunchback as some say? The poor man!"

Eleanor poured her guest some tea. "I do not believe he is," she said, "for I have seen him riding on horseback before, and he always appeared to sit straight and tall in the saddle."

"Did you never see him at church?"

"Not after the accident. The Cartwrights did not attend church."

"Not attend church!"

Eleanor laughed at her friend's horrified expression. "Well, not with any regularity. I do recall one instance in my youth when Mr. Cartwright came with his son. He made the poor boy wear what equated to a woman's mourning bonnet, in order to hide his face. And after the sermon, Mr. Cartwright stood up and publicly berated the minister for his hypocrisy in preaching temperance, when he claimed that Father Montierth drank himself sick every other night."

"No!"

"Yes. And then he turned on the congregation and lambasted every last one of them. Needless to say, there were some harsh words flung back at him as well, and he never set foot in the church again."

"But what became of the boy? Where was his mother?"

Eleanor shrugged. "She died, and Albert was shut up in the manor with his father."

"Did Mr. Cartwright never let him leave?"

"Whether Mr. Cartwright did not allow his son to leave, or his son chose not to venture out on his own, I cannot say. But as I said before, I have seen him riding in the woods near here, before he went away for good. Only from a distance, mind. But I daresay the townsfolk rarely, if ever, saw him."

Mrs. Lewis looked thoughtful. "Did no one ever visit them? As their nearest neighbors and closest peers, were you not on friendly terms with them?"

"I believe my mother tried. She and Mrs. Cartwright were friends, and she was devastated after the accident. But Mr. Cartwright must have turned her away." Eleanor shook her head, frowning. "I cannot recall exactly. I was still so young, and my own mother entered her confinement soon after... and then she died as well."

Mrs. Lewis reached over and squeezed her hand, and Eleanor smiled in gratitude. "Aside from that, I do not believe anyone else made an effort," she added.

"I daresay you can make the effort now."

Eleanor looked with such alarm at her friend that Mrs. Lewis laughed. "Come now, Miss Eves! Surely Mr. Cartwright is not so frightening that you wish to avoid him?"

"I believe it is Mr. Cartwright that wishes to avoid all of us," Eleanor hedged.

"Well, I for one plan to speak with Mr. Lewis directly, and take the opportunity of calling on Mr. Cartwright before he disappears again."

True to her word, Mrs. Lewis and the minister went to call the very next day, but as Mr. Cartwright was engaged in business with his steward, they were unable to see him. When Mrs. Lewis confessed to her friend several days later that he had not returned their visit, Eleanor raised her brow as if to say "I told you so."

October was drawing to a close, and with the holiday bazaar only a few weeks away, Eleanor was busily engaged in her preparations. All the members of the little parish must be visited, and their pledges secured. Many of them would be donating items, but even those who were not would still come to the church to make purchases and visit with their neighbors. The holiday bazaar had morphed into an event half charity, half party, and no one missed it who was possibly able to attend.

The town of Littleton was very small. It had only one main road, with a handful of businesses and a few houses stationed along it. Most of the families in the neighborhood lived on farms, and were thus more spread out. Because of the distance between houses, Eleanor normally took the carriage on her visits. Today, however, her father and brother had taken it into Norwich to pick up the new furniture for the drawing room. Since she would thus be required to walk, Eleanor decided to visit only the Smiths, and be home in time for dinner.

Pulling on her gloves, Eleanor emerged from the house and looked down the lane, contemplating which direction to take. If she cut through the Cartwright estate, it was only three miles to the Smiths' farm, while going around meant nearly double that distance. She glanced at the sky. It was cloudy, as usual, with only a light breeze, but at this time of year, the weather could change at a moment's notice. Not wanting to get stuck in an early winter storm, especially on foot, she decided to take the shorter route.

The woods and meadows surrounding Cartwright Manor were some of the finest in the county. As children, Eleanor and Nathaniel used to romp and frolic all through them; climbing trees, splashing in the streams, and collecting berries. When they were discovered by the elder Mr. Cartwright, he had ranted and raved about "miscreant children" and expressly forbidden them from trespassing again. Of course, they had not obeyed this injunction, but only took greater care to prevent themselves from being caught. Eleanor knew the park extremely well, and by keeping to the westernmost path, she knew she could pass through to the other side and be at the Smiths' home within the hour.

With her full skirts sweeping through the dried leaves, she allowed her mind to dwell on the new furniture that would soon fill her drawing room. She had chosen rose-colored drapes, and a beautiful new settee to match. The floor would be covered in a new beige carpet, with an ornate floral border and blossoms scattered throughout the design. After commissioning the carpet, it had proven too expensive to refurnish the entire room, so some of the chairs and end tables were being refinished and given fresh upholstery. She was excited to see it all come together, and hoped it might be ready for guests by Christmas.

Eleanor was so wrapped up in her thoughts, she did not realize she had missed the bend in the path, until a sudden turn brought the manor into view. Chiding herself for not paying closer attention, she quickly withdrew back the way she had come, only to hear the sound of a horse and rider coming towards her. Oh, what wretched luck! She was caught, and with nowhere else to turn, she pressed her hands to her stomach and waited.

As she suspected, the approaching horseman turned out to be none other than Albert Cartwright. Though ashamed at being caught on his property without an invitation, Eleanor could not deny the curiosity she felt in seeing him. She was standing off the path under a tree, and his horse passed directly in front of her. Looking up at his face, she gasped, one hand flying to her mouth.

Startled, Albert pulled his horse to a stop several paces from where she stood. His surprise at finding her was nearly as great as Eleanor's embarrassment, and for a moment neither of them spoke. At last he broke the silence.

"Forgive me," he said, touching the brim of his hat. "To whom do I have the honor of addressing?"

Eleanor curtsied. "Miss Eleanor Eves," she said, trying not to stare. "We are your neighbors to the east, at Edgewood Park."

She glanced again at his face, but almost immediately looked away. A long scar ran from his left temple down across his cheek, cutting across his mouth before tracking down the middle of his chin. Though his eye had not been injured, the puckered skin from the scar caused it to pull down in the outer corner. His mouth was disfigured as well, and though the right side of his face appeared perfectly calm, the left seemed drawn into a permanent grimace. The effect was so alarming, that a shiver of fear coursed through her, even though Eleanor knew he was harmless.

"I am sorry if I startled you," he said. "I did not expect to see anyone today."

Eleanor blushed. "It is I who must apologize. Forgive me for trespassing on your property, sir; I should not have taken the liberty."

"There is no harm in walking through the woods," he said. "I quite enjoy them myself, though I prefer to ride."

He looked down at her as if waiting for a response, and she timidly lifted her eyes to his face. His horse had stepped closer to her than before, and she could now see the angry folds of scarred flesh in greater detail. Eleanor shuddered involuntarily, and she saw his shoulders stiffen in response.

"Forgive me," he said, pulling on the reins to make his horse step back. "I can see that you wish to be alone. Please accept my wishes for a pleasant day."

He touched the brim of his hat once more and turned away, leading his horse in the opposite direction. Guilt washed over her as Eleanor watched his retreating figure, and she almost called out to him… but the moment passed, and he was gone. Slowly, she turned herself around and made her way back down the path, puzzling over the man she had just encountered.

21

Though her first meeting with Albert Cartwright had left her with more questions than answers, two thoughts pressed upon her mind: First, that he was far more genteel than she had anticipated—his civility and manner of speaking had surprised her almost as much as his appearance did. And second, that the scars he bore upon his face were even more grotesque than she could have imagined.

Chapter 4

Albert replayed his meeting with Eleanor Eves again and again in his mind. Surprise, curiosity, horror, disgust; he had read them on her face as clearly as if she had spoken her feelings aloud. It was nothing he had not encountered before, and yet, it upset him far more than he cared to admit. Usually he ignored the impolite stares and whispered assumptions that followed him. But Miss Eves's reaction had resurrected feelings of anger and despair which he had not felt in a long time, and it was upon this—his own response to her reaction—that his mind dwelt.

He sighed, rubbing the back of his neck. Perhaps it was not Miss Eves herself, but what she represented that upset him. All his life he had been shunned and despised: first by his father, and then by society. Living under Franklin Cartwright's thumb meant that Albert had rarely encountered the townspeople of Littleton, and his meeting with Miss Eves was the first of its kind in over a decade. Why he had expected a warmer, more receptive welcome made no sense at all, especially from a pretty, genteel woman like Miss Eves. No one of her class had ever looked at him with anything other than abhorrence—why should he have expected anything different from her?

When the bell rang an hour later, Albert was still trying to force his thoughts away from Miss Eves.

"Master Albert, Father Lewis and his wife are here to see you," his housekeeper announced.

Albert sighed. He had hoped to send whomever it was away, but he knew that propriety demanded that a man of the cloth should always be received when possible.

"Tell them I will be with them shortly."

"Yes, sir."

Taking his walking stick, Albert leaned against it and limped down the hall to the drawing room. His cane made a sharp *clack* against the stone as he walked, announcing his approach like the ringing of a leper's bell.

Upon entering the cavernous room, Albert observed a middle-aged man with graying hair seated beside a rather plain-looking woman. They both looked up at his entrance, and Father Lewis stood. "How do you, Mr. Cartwright?" he said.

"How do you do, Father? I hope I have not kept you waiting long."

"Not at all."

The gentlemen took their seats, and Albert turned his attention to the minister's wife. He could feel her gaze upon his face, and was prepared to see her revulsion when their eyes met. But as he looked at her, he saw only mild curiosity in her smiling face. No malice, no horror. The sight both surprised and unnerved him.

"We understand that you are lately arrived, Mr. Cartwright," she said pleasantly, "and we wished to welcome you to the neighborhood."

"Thank you."

"You have our condolences, as well," Father Lewis said, "on the passing of your father."

Albert shifted in his seat. "I mourn him out of propriety alone. But thank you."

Father Lewis was visibly surprised at this response, but his wife looked only thoughtful.

"I am sorry that I was not here for the services," Albert continued. "I was in Austria when I received the news he had died, and came as quickly as I could. Everything went smoothly, I trust?"

"Yes, of course."

"I am glad to hear it."

The gentlemen lapsed into silence, and Mrs. Lewis took up the conversation. "I understand you have been out of the country for many years," she said.

"That is correct."

"Do you plan to stay long on this visit?" Father Lewis asked.

"I certainly hope not. My present business requires that I remain in Norfolk another week or two, but I shall be gone again as soon as it is finished."

"It is a shame you will not be staying longer," Mrs. Lewis said. "Your presence would surely have been a welcome addition to the neighborhood."

Albert laughed humorlessly. "You are mistaken, Mrs. Lewis. I have never been welcome anywhere, least of all in Littleton."

Father Lewis frowned. "Surely you have felt welcome in your own home?"

Albert regarded the couple in front of him. Father Lewis looked every inch the minister: solemn eyes, gentle smile, penetrating gaze. His wife, though plain, had a pleasant air about her, and as he studied her face, she smiled, her eyes crinkling at the corners.

"How long have you been in the parish, if I might ask?" Albert said.

"Three years."

"Then you knew my father?"

The Lewises exchanged glances. "I confess to have only known him in reputation," Father Lewis said. "He never let me enter the house, and he never came to church."

"Well, there you have it." Albert smiled grimly, the scar along his face twisting it into a grimace. "My father made me feel about as welcome as he did you. He treated me like a monster, and the people of Littleton were not very welcoming, either."

"Do you mean to say," cried Mrs. Lewis, "that the townspeople despised you, merely because of your appearance?"

Albert shrugged. "I rarely went into town. When I did, the people treated me as if I were diseased. I saw their looks and heard their comments. I was not welcome there, any more than I was welcome here."

The pity he saw in her face did not anger him, but it signaled the end of their conversation. He sighed, wishing they could have talked of other things. Father Lewis seemed like the sort of man he could have a real conversation with, and Mrs. Lewis... well, he did not know what to make of her, but she certainly intrigued him. He would not converse, however, with someone moved to pity him. Those conversations spiraled in only one direction, and he refused to follow where it led.

Leaning on his cane, Albert got to his feet. "Thank you for coming to call. I sincerely appreciate your interest in my welfare, but do not trouble yourself over me. I will be gone again soon enough, and your little parish will be as before."

The Lewises knew they were being dismissed, and though they smiled as they bid him good day, he could not help feeling that they were disappointed. "Perhaps we shall see you at church on Sunday," Mrs. Lewis said with a hopeful smile.

Albert's brow furrowed. "Mrs. Lewis," he said, looking at her curiously. "I do not believe I have ever met a lady quite like you, if you will forgive my saying so."

Her surprised look melted away in a laugh. "If you mean that as a compliment, then there is nothing to forgive," she said.

"Indeed, I do."

"In that case, I thank you. And I hope you will indeed join us for worship services."

Albert made no reply.

"Good day, Mr. Cartwright," Father Lewis said. "You seem a very pleasant fellow, and I look forward to seeing you again."

He extended his hand, and Albert, surprised but pleased, shook it heartily. The Lewises bid him good day again, and he was left alone, wondering what on earth had just happened.

Chapter 5

Meetings in the Littleton chapel were quiet affairs, so the arrival of Albert Cartwright the next Sunday certainly made a sensation. As far as anyone was aware, the elder Mr. Cartwright had never set foot in the building after that fateful day when he castigated the town. When his son, therefore, turned up in time for the meeting, and sat attentively in a pew during the whole of Father Lewis's sermon, the entire neighborhood was thrown into an uproar.

"Do you see him? Mr. Cartwright is actually at church!"

"He doesn't look like a hunchback to me."

"The poor man! Did you see his scar?"

"I wonder where he's been all these years?"

"His father never came to church, you know."

"He would almost be handsome, if it weren't for his face."

"Do you know how long he plans to stay?"

Eleanor attempted to ignore the whispering of her neighbors, but she could not concentrate on anything Father Lewis was saying. From the corner of her eye, she could see Mr. Cartwright's tall, stately form, sitting near the front in a side pew. In vain she tried to keep her mind on the text upon which Father Lewis was expostulating, but her eyes kept shifting to see what Mr. Cartwright was doing.

His eyes never once strayed from the pulpit.

When at last the sermon was over, Eleanor saw him rise to his feet, leaning heavily upon a cane. Hmm. She did not realize he was lame. Sitting astride his horse, he'd had no need for a walking stick.

"Considering apologizing to our neighbor, eh?"

Eleanor turned at Nathaniel's voice, her face flushing. "It is not *my* fault the man startled me on my walk. And no, I am not. I was merely curious—I never supposed he would come to church."

"Neither did anyone else, it seems."

It was true. An excited hum had filled the chapel, and many of their friends were casting furtive glances in the direction of Mr. Cartwright, who was speaking with the minister and his wife. Eleanor, however, did not wish to hear any more of what her neighbors had to say. Their shocked whispers and repulsed comments made her feel ill, and guilt for her own initial reaction settled once more in her gut. Taking her brother's arm, she turned towards the door.

"Miss Eves! Mr. Eves!"

They turned to see Mrs. Lewis hailing them from the front of the room. Beside her, Albert glanced in their direction before looking away.

Nathaniel and Eleanor exchanged looks before redirecting their steps. Mrs. Lewis smiled as they came up beside her.

"I wonder if you have been introduced to your recently returned neighbor, Mr. Albert Cartwright," she said.

"How do you do, Mr. Cartwright?" Nathaniel said with a slight bow.

"How do you do?" came the reply. Then, glancing down at Eleanor, he added, "How do you do, Miss Eves?"

Eleanor, who had been looking at the floor, drew a breath and glanced up. He was looking directly at her, and whether it was the softer light or the closer distance she did not know, but the disfigurement on his face seemed neither as pronounced, nor as disturbing as she remembered. Relieved, she offered a tentative smile.

"Good day, Mr. Cartwright."

"Miss Eves, is your father unwell?" Father Lewis asked.

Eleanor turned to answer the minister. "He had a headache this morning, and chose to stay home and rest."

"I am sorry to hear it. I hope he recovers quickly."

"Thank you, sir."

"I have just been saying to Mr. Cartwright," Father Lewis continued, "that though he is only in the country for a short time, he ought to take advantage of the time of year and enjoy a bit of sport."

"By all means, Mr. Cartwright," Nathaniel said, "you ought to take the advice of the good Father. I daresay there is a fair deal of grouse in your woods."

"I am only here on business," Albert said, rather stiffly.

"And what is hunting but a bit of pleasurable business?" Nathaniel grinned.

Albert's expression changed, and after a short pause, he said, "Very well. If you will come and shoot with me, I should be glad to have a bit of sport."

Nathaniel looked taken aback, but he readily agreed. The next morning was decided upon, and the parties bid each other good day.

"He seems a pleasant enough fellow," Nathaniel said to Eleanor as they walked outside. "But you are right—that scar along his face is quite a sight to see."

Eleanor shuddered. "It certainly is," she said, climbing inside their carriage. "Though it is not as terrible as I remember it being. Perhaps it was thrown into sharper relief when he was upon his horse."

"Perhaps. It appears he has a crooked leg as well."

Eleanor looked out the carriage window, to where Albert Cartwright was mounting his horse. He swung himself up with practiced ease, and soon rode smoothly away, sitting straight and tall.

He did not look back.

"Good shot, Eves!"

Albert and Nathaniel watched as a servant fetched the bird he had brought down. "You have a very good eye," Albert said.

Nathaniel grinned. "Thank you. I used to practice every day when I was growing up."

31

"And do you still?"

"Not while I am at school."

"You are at school, then?"

"Yes, at Cambridge."

"Ah, poor fellow," Albert said sorrowfully. "Oxford is the better school, you know."

Nathaniel barked a laugh, and Albert smiled with half of his face. It felt foreign—he was not accustomed to smiling much. Nor was he accustomed to feeling so at ease in the presence of another person. Nathaniel was likely ten years his junior, but he spoke with such affability, and looked with such indifference upon Albert's malformed face, that Albert could not help but wish to know him better. He and Mrs. Lewis seemed cut from the same cloth.

"Come, let us take some refreshment," Albert said, gesturing to the house.

Nathaniel fell into step beside him, shortening his stride to accommodate the other man's uneven gait. "Tell me," Albert said, "how do you like it at Cambridge?"

"I like it well enough," Nathaniel shrugged, "but I shall be glad when I am through."

"Will you be entering a profession?"

"No, I will return home when I am finished."

"Have you traveled much?"

"Not outside of Britain."

"Would you like to?"

"Perhaps. But the duties I owe to my family must first be fulfilled."

They entered the house then, and made their way through the

cavernous entrance hall to the drawing room. Cartwright Manor was an old stone edifice with soaring ceilings and echoing hallways, giving it a rather cathedralesque appearance. The drawing room had been made more comfortable by the addition of thick carpets and large tapestries, but the narrow, leaded windows did little to let in what natural light there was. Albert lit several large candelabras before calling a servant to bring them some refreshment.

"Tell me, Cartwright," Nathaniel said, sitting down in a chair. "What have you been doing with yourself these last few years?"

"A bit of everything," Albert said, limping to the sideboard and pulling out some glasses. "I have done a great deal of traveling."

"Where have you gone?"

"All over the continent. France, Belgium, Italy, Spain… wherever my interests have led me."

"What sort of interests?"

Albert paused, considering. What could he say? He left England a lonely, bitter man, and in every place he visited, he desperately sought for the companionship and sense of belonging he had never had. But that felt too personal to share.

"Forgive me," Albert said, realizing that too much time had passed without answering Nathaniel's question. "I was lost in thought for a moment." He filled a tumbler and handed it to his guest. "You asked what sort of interests have led me around the world, is that right?"

"Yes."

Albert took a sip from his own glass. "My interests have varied. When I left England I did not know exactly what I was

33

searching for, so I wandered from place to place, hoping I would find it."

"And did you?"

Albert hesitated. "I found a great many things, in many different places."

"But not what you were looking for." It was a statement, not a question.

"I found God," Albert shrugged, "and that was something I did not have before."

Nathaniel nodded, and the men fell silent. Soon a servant arrived with a large tray of cold meats, preserved fruit, bread, and cheese, and the gentlemen eagerly filled their plates. Their conversation was light and sporadic while they dined, and at the end of it, Nathaniel sat back, a satisfied smile on his face.

"I thank you for the invitation to shoot with you today," he said. "I cannot tell you when I passed a day more pleasantly than this."

"Nor I," Albert found himself saying.

"It is a pity you will not be staying in the country much longer."

"Yes, a great pity. But there is nothing for me here. My business is almost finished, and then it will be time for me to go."

"A man such as yourself certainly has the right to go whenever and wherever he chooses, but if I might be so bold, why must you go?"

"I just told you—there is nothing for me here."

"And is there something for you in Vienna? Prague? Stockholm? God is as much here as he is there."

Albert leaned back in his chair, rubbing his chin. "Why does it matter to you?" he said.

Nathaniel shrugged, his eyes twinkling. "It does not matter insofar as your own happiness is concerned, I suppose. But if we are to be friends, you ought to know that I am a horribly selfish being. I like you, Cartwright, and would like to shoot with you again. Provided you extend another invitation, that is." He winked, and Albert laughed, which felt even more foreign than smiling.

"You are a cheeky young devil," he said. "No wonder they did not want you at Oxford."

Nathaniel threw back his head and laughed, and Albert chuckled with him.

"You see, Cartwright?" Nathaniel said, "you simply must stay. I shall die of boredom if you do not, and then my death would be upon *your* head."

"Very well," Albert replied, still chuckling. "I shall stay. But only for a few weeks."

Nathaniel grinned, and Albert shook his head, wondering what was happening to him.

Chapter 6

The first week in November found Eleanor supervising the completion of the drawing room. The new carpet had been laid, and the furniture which would fill the room was staged in the parlor. A handful of servants carried in tables and chairs and moved them around as she directed—first one way, then another. Just when she would get one seating arrangement situated to her liking, another piece of furniture was brought in that disrupted the whole thing.

She was not expecting any visitors, and was therefore very much surprised when the housekeeper entered the room and announced that Mr. Albert Cartwright was waiting in the entry.

"Albert Cartwright?"

"Yes, miss."

"Did he ask for me?"

"No, miss—he only said he was come to call on the family."

Eleanor walked slowly down the corridor, counting her steps and her breaths in order to remain calm. She felt ridiculous admitting to herself that the man's face frightened her, and she did not want to embarrass or upset him again. Turning the corner, she saw him standing in the center of the entrance hall. He heard her approach and turned, his face registering surprise.

"Miss Eves," he said, removing his hat. "How do you do?"

Eleanor curtsied. "How do you do, Mr. Cartwright." She smiled timidly at him, but he did not smile back.

"Forgive me," Albert continued, with a look of confusion, "but your housekeeper said nothing of your being alone. Is your brother not at home?"

"No, Nathaniel is visiting with friends this morning."

"And your father?"

"At the parsonage."

"I see."

The awkward silence that followed this exchange was heavy with unspoken assumptions. Eleanor waited expectantly for Albert to say something else, but when he did not, she asked, "Was there something you wished to speak to my brother or father about?"

"No, I was simply making a neighborly call. I had no particular business to attend to."

Silence fell once more. After a few moments, Eleanor asked if he would like to come in and sit down. This time he attempted to smile, but the scar twisted his lips into a smirk.

"Thank you, but I do not wish to intrude. I am sure you are busy with your preparations for the bazaar."

There was a pause. "How do you know about that?" she asked.

"It was all I heard about at church. Well, that, and how shocking my presence there was."

Eleanor gasped, and he chuckled. "Do not worry, Miss Eves. I did not hear anything from *you* on that subject."

The color rose in Eleanor's cheeks. "I would never..." she stammered.

"Forgive me," Albert said abruptly, his face serious. "I did not mean to imply that you would speak ill of anyone. In fact, from what I hear of your work in the parish, you are probably the least likely of the town to gossip about me behind my back."

"I am no saint, Mr. Cartwright," Eleanor said, looking down.

"Nor am I, Miss Eves," he replied.

The silence grew between them, and Eleanor wondered if he, like she, was thinking of their first meeting. Shame welled up inside of her, and she glanced up at him. He was looking away, out one of the windows, the scar across his face standing between them like a stone wall.

She knew not what to say.

"I believe I have taken enough of your time already this morning," he said at last, turning to face her. "Please accept my compliments, and extend them to your father and brother as well. I look forward to calling upon your family at a more opportune time."

He bowed, and without another word, left the house.

Eleanor walked slowly back to the drawing room, but she could not bring herself to finish the task which had been interrupted. Dismissing the servants, she sought refuge in her chambers. She paced in front of the window, trying to determine why her heart was so sick, and what she could possibly do to make it better.

A knock sounded on her bedroom door and she turned, expecting to see one of the maids. Instead, Nathaniel opened the door and stuck his head in.

"Eleanor? Is everything all right?"

"Of course. Why do you ask?"

He frowned, coming into the room. "The drawing room and parlor are both in disarray. I thought you were putting them back together this morning? Did you run into some trouble?"

Eleanor sighed. "Not exactly, no. But Albert Cartwright came to call."

Nathaniel's eyebrows shot up. "He did? Did he give a reason?"

"No—he said only that he wished to make a neighborly visit."

"That is wonderful!" her brother cried. Eleanor looked perplexed.

"Why is that wonderful?" she asked.

"Nora, don't you see? The man is reaching out—*he* came *here!* Can you imagine how hard that must have been for him?" He paused. "Did you invite him in?"

She huffed. "Of course I invited him in! But he declined, saying he would call upon the family at a more opportune time."

Sitting down on the edge of the bed, Nathaniel looked up at her. "Nora, can I ask you a question? I would like your honest answer."

"Of course."

"Are you frightened of Mr. Cartwright?"

Eleanor hesitated. "A little bit, yes. That scar..." She shuddered. "The poor man."

Nathaniel shook his head. "He does not want your pity, Nora.

Pity will drive him away, and I want him to stay."

She looked at him curiously. "Why?"

He shrugged. "I like him. Is not that reason enough?"

"I suppose so. But Nathan, why did you ask me if I was frightened of him?"

"Because I want your help with something."

"Oh?"

"I want you to talk to him. Really talk to him. Get to know all about him if you can."

"Why me?"

"Because I am already trying to break through his shell, but I cannot do it alone. He told me he found God, but I am not convinced that is all he went looking for when he left."

"What do you mean?"

"Think about it, Nora; he has no family, no friends, and as prickly as he is at times, I think he rather wishes that he did."

Eleanor sat down beside him, arranging her skirts. "Why do you not ask Father Lewis to help you?" she said, not meeting his gaze. "He is the minister, after all."

Nathaniel rolled his eyes. "If I wanted Father Lewis's help, I would have asked Father Lewis."

"But why me?"

"Cartwright grew up without a mother, did he not? He needs a woman's gentling influence in his life, someone with true Christian charity—and I can think of no one better suited to the task than yourself."

"Mrs. Lewis?"

"Mrs. Lewis is all the way in town, and you are right here. Besides, it will be less awkward for me to work with you than to work with Mrs. Lewis."

She narrowed her eyes at him, wondering what he was up to. His smiling face looked far too innocent, but when he said nothing else, she finally sighed.

"Very well," she said. "I will try."

"That's the spirit! I knew I could count on you, Nora."

"You shall be counting the favors you owe me before long," she said, feigning irritation.

"One day you will thank me, Nora, you'll see."

"I highly doubt that."

He laughed, and she shoved him playfully out the door.

Chapter 7

The next day, Eleanor coerced her brother into helping her put the parlor and drawing room back in order. A half dozen servants were called in to arrange the remaining furniture, and soon both rooms were set to rights.

"I certainly hope you do not plan to do this very often," Nathaniel said, dropping into a chair.

"Of course I shall," his sister teased. "I intend to make over the bedrooms when you next come home to visit."

He groaned, and Eleanor laughed.

"Well, it is done at last, and I daresay it looks very well," he said.

"Thank you," Eleanor beamed. "It is a very handsome room, and finished just in time—Mrs. Lewis and the other ladies will be arriving this afternoon for a quilting bee. The quilt we are working on will be donated to the bazaar, so naturally I offered to act as hostess for the event."

Nathaniel chuckled. "Cutting things a bit close, are you not?"

Eleanor tossed her head, her green eyes sparkling. "Nonsense! I still have two hours to spare."

The ladies of the parish began arriving shortly after dinner. Mrs. Lewis came with two other women, who lived near her in town, and they brought a large quilting frame with them. Mrs. Sotherby came with the quilt, and several others joined them before long. Soon the fabric and batting were stretched tight and the women gathered around to sew.

"What do you think of Mr. Cartwright's return?" one of the ladies asked.

"A bit late, if you ask me," another replied. "Why, he wasn't even here for his own father's funeral!"

"Do you blame him? The elder Mr. Cartwright was a right old devil. I wouldn't be surprised if the scars on Mr. Cartwright's face are from his own father."

A general outcry followed these words, but the lady nodded gravely. "Aye. Franklin Cartwright had a nasty temper. Who's to say he didn't maim the child during a fit of anger?"

"You know perfectly well that is not what happened, Augusta," her neighbor said, frowning. "It was that accident with the carriage—the same one as took his mother's life."

"Poor woman! She was such a pretty thing, and she loved that little boy something fierce."

"I never knew Mrs. Cartwright," Eleanor said, knotting the thread on her needle. "What was she like?"

Mrs. Sotherby looked up from her place in the circle. "Henrietta? You knew her, didn't you?"

All eyes turned to the elderly woman sitting beside Mrs. Lewis. Henrietta Jones had been the midwife for the town as long as Eleanor could remember. Littleton was too small to have a doctor, so whenever there was an ailment, illness, or baby coming along, she was the one they called upon.

The old woman sighed. "Ah, Marguerite. She was a doe-like creature, more sweet and gentle than most. Franklin Cartwright simply doted on her."

"I remember when he brought her home, a new bride," another voice chimed in.

"Aye. And then she went and had the baby, and my, if ever a mother loved a child more!" Mrs. Jones said.

"It was such a pity when she died."

"What happened?" Mrs. Lewis asked.

"Well, there was an accident, you see. Franklin Cartwright wasn't with them, but Marguerite and the boy—he was about seven or eight, I believe—were carried away by a runaway horse."

Nods and murmurs filled the room, and Mrs. Jones continued. "Naturally, I went over as soon as I got word. Mr. Cartwright was nearly mad with grief. He'd sent for the doctor in Norwich, of course, but I could see plain as day there was nothing to be done for her; she was already gone. He wouldn't listen to me, though—insisted on waiting for the doctor.

"When I asked about the boy, he didn't even seem to care about him! All he said was 'Look him over if you wish,' so I did." She shuddered. "He was in a bad state, I tell you. I thought we'd lose him, too. He's the one that needed the doctor, but when I tried to insist on the urgency of his wounds, Franklin Cartwright flew into a rage." She sat up straight, looking around at the women, whose eyes were all fixed on her face. "He threw a pot at me, and told me to get out and never come back."

Cries of outrage and shock followed her words, as if the women had never heard the story before. She nodded. "I ran out of that house, I did, and I never went back, just like he said."

"Sarah Jane worked over there before my little Ruthie," Mrs. Harrison piped up. "She said the servants were ordered not to speak a single word about the late Mrs. Cartwright, or to even mention the deformities of the boy."

"Did the doctor ever come?" someone asked.

"Don't know," Mrs. Harrison shrugged. "Sarah Jane said the boy was shut away—said Mr. Cartwright tended him himself."

"Neglected him, more like," another woman said.

A murmur of assent filled the room. Mrs. Lewis looked up from her needle. "Is that why Mr. Cartwright went away?"

"Seems likely. He left around the time he came of age," Mrs. Sotherby said.

"Surely his father was not cruel to him?"

"No one can say for sure—we never saw them much together."

"And they did not attend church?"

The women laughed. "Land sakes, no!" Mrs. Bryant said, speaking for them all. "That's why it was such a shock to see Mr. Cartwright there on Sunday."

Mrs. Jones turned to Eleanor. "Your mothers were friends, were they not, Miss Eves? What else do you know about Mr. Cartwright?"

All eyes turned to face her. "Not much more than has been

said already. But my brother seems to have taken a fancy to him, so perhaps we shall learn something else of him in time."

A few quiet conversations broke out, and soon a general hum filled the room. After an hour, Eleanor called for refreshment, and trays of tea and biscuits were brought in. The women ate while they talked, asking each other about their families and inquiring after the health of their neighbors. A wave of affection swelled in Eleanor's heart as she looked around the room. The women before her were more than her friends and neighbors; they were like family.

When the quilt had been finished and bound, and all the tarts and sandwiches enjoyed, Eleanor bid good day to each of her guests.

"Thank you so much for coming," she said to Mrs. Jones, clasping her hands.

"My fingers aren't as nimble as they once were, but 'tis good to gather together. Good day, Miss Eves."

At last the only guest remaining was Mrs. Lewis. Eleanor turned to her as the servants came in to clean up after the gathering.

"Well! I believe the day has been a great success. We finished a beautiful quilt, and I think everyone had an enjoyable time."

"The afternoon was lovely, my dear. You are an excellent hostess."

"Would you like to stay for supper? We can send word to the parsonage for Father Lewis to join us."

"I would be delighted. But do not bother sending word to my husband—he has holed himself up in his library with a new text and shan't emerge until his sermon is finished. I know the routine well," Mrs. Lewis said with a smile.

The ladies retired to the parlor, to rest before the meal. As they walked down the hallway, Eleanor could hear voices in the billiard room. Curious, she knocked on the door.

Abruptly the voices ceased, and Nathaniel appeared in the doorway.

"Nora!" he said. Then, looking over her shoulder, he added, "How do you, Mrs. Lewis?"

"How do you do, Mr. Eves," Mrs. Lewis smiled. "Eleanor, I shall wait for you in the parlor."

Eleanor nodded, watching her go. Turning back to her brother, she frowned. "I heard voices from the hallway. Nathan, is someone here?"

"Albert Cartwright. He stopped by while you were entertaining and we have spent the afternoon together. I have invited him to sup with us." Grinning, he added, "I thought it would be a chance for you to make good on your promise."

Eleanor rolled her eyes, and Nathaniel laughed, turning back into the room. Placing her hands on her stomach, Eleanor drew a breath. She could do this. She *would* do this.

When it was nearly time for supper, she and Mrs. Lewis entered the drawing room to find Albert Cartwright speaking with her father and brother. He turned and bowed at their approach.

"How do you do, Miss Eves? Mrs. Lewis?"

"How do you do Mr. Cartwright?" the ladies said in chorus.

"It is a pity that your husband did not accompany you today," Mr. Eves said to Mrs. Lewis as everyone went into the dining room. "With my daughter working on the bazaar and my son out with friends, I have felt very much neglected."

Mrs. Lewis smiled. "I am sure he would have liked to come, but he is preparing his sermon for Sunday and has not yet emerged from his library."

"Father Lewis is quite the orator," Albert said after everyone had taken their seats. "His sermons are some of the best I have heard."

Eleanor took a sip from her glass. Albert Cartwright had been attending church elsewhere? Nathaniel had mentioned that Albert had "found God," but the news still surprised her.

"Are you a very religious man, Mr. Cartwright?" Mrs. Lewis asked.

"I believe in the existence of Deity, if that is what you mean. And I have worshiped in some of the most magnificent chapels this world has ever seen."

"Really! Have you been to Westminster? And Notre Dame?"

He smiled. "And St. Peter's. Yes."

"I have only been to Westminster myself," Mrs. Lewis said. "But I would love to see the great cathedrals and houses of worship on the continent."

"It sounds like you have traveled extensively," Mr. Eves said, taking a spoonful of soup.

"Yes. When I left here eight years ago, I determined to see as much of the world as I could. I have been very fortunate in my ability to do so."

Eleanor caught Nathaniel's eye, who jerked his head in Albert's direction. She took a deep breath.

"How lucky you have been to travel so extensively," she said to Albert. "For my part, I prefer to stay at home. There is no place in the world I would rather be than at Edgewood Park."

Albert regarded her thoughtfully. "Have you traveled much yourself, Miss Eves?"

"No, not at all. The furthest I have ever been from home is London."

He was clearly surprised. "Then how can you say that you prefer Edgewood to anywhere else? Have you no desire to see the beauty found beyond this county?"

Eleanor shook her head. "I am sure the world holds more beauty than I could see in a lifetime. But beauty is not what I long for, and it is not what I consider most important."

Albert paused, considering her words. "Familiarity, then?"

"Of a sort. What endears Edgewood Park to my heart—and all of Littleton, for that matter—is the people."

"I can see your reasoning," Albert said after a pause. "Though I have never shared the same sentiment, either here, or anywhere else."

Mrs. Lewis looked up from her plate. "I know you have never felt quite comfortable here, Mr. Cartwright, but there is a cure for that, you know."

Albert stiffened. "My father employed the most skilled physicians and surgeons in the country, Mrs. Lewis. There is nothing that can be done for me."

"Good heavens, I did not mean that!" Mrs. Lewis cried in mortification. "There is no reason to be ashamed of your scars, or to be concerned about your appearance." She blushed in agitation. "I only meant that there is something you can do to feel more like a part of the community."

He raised one eyebrow.

"I would venture a guess," she continued, forging ahead, "that the reason you did not feel as though you belonged in Littleton, was because you cared so little about the people here. If you were to take it into your heart to get to know them, *really* know them, I think you might find that you belong here very much indeed. And the best way to get to know someone," she smiled benevolently, "is to serve them."

"Serve them!"

"I do not mean that you should be their servant," Mrs. Lewis said in a rush, lest she offend him again. "I only meant to *help* them. Care for them. Show them that you are concerned for their well-being; for the well-being of the entire town."

"Forgive me, Mrs. Lewis," Albert said, "but I do not think the people of Littleton would like to let me into their lives. They can hardly stand the sight of me."

"Perhaps not at the moment. But have you tried speaking with them about it?"

He looked taken aback. "Of course not."

"Then let me propose a little experiment," Mrs. Lewis said cheerfully. "I am sure you are aware of the charity bazaar that Miss Eves puts on for the town every year?"

An alarm went off in Eleanor's head. What was Mrs. Lewis doing?

"I have heard of it, yes," Albert said, narrowing his eyes.

"Miss Eves has become so adept at knowing the needs of the community, that I can think of nothing better suited to help you navigate your way into their hearts than in assisting her with the bazaar."

Eleanor's gasp was hidden by Nathaniel's guffaw. "Splendid idea, Mrs. Lewis! And I daresay my sister could use the help.

What do you say, Nora?"

Eleanor looked helplessly from her brother to her friend, who were both grinning at her. "I am sure Mr. Cartwright has better things to do than help with my bazaar."

"Nonsense! Cartwright was just telling me this afternoon he is afraid he shall die of boredom if he remains here much longer."

Albert allowed himself a small smile. "That may be a bit of an exaggeration, Eves. I believe I was merely comparing the relative differences between life in the country and life in town."

Nathaniel shrugged good-humoredly, and Mrs. Lewis looked expectantly at Eleanor. "Well, my dear? What do you say?"

Desperate, Eleanor looked to her father, but he merely raised his eyebrows, wiping his lips with a cloth to hide a smile. At last, with no ally beside her, Eleanor looked across the table at Albert. His eyes were guarded, and she wondered what he was thinking.

She placed a hand on her stomach, drawing a slow breath. Smiling timidly, she said, "Nathaniel is right—I could use some help. I still have several visits to make, and would be glad of the company. And I need someone to rally the menfolk into helping set up the church for the event."

For a moment, their eyes locked. Eleanor met his gaze, determined not to look away or let her fears and concerns show in her own expression. Finally, Albert's face relaxed.

"If you would be desirous of my company, Miss Eves, I would be happy to be of assistance."

"Wonderful!" Mrs. Lewis cried, clapping her hands together. She beamed at Eleanor, who forced another smile.

What in heaven's name had she just agreed to?

Chapter 8

Albert Cartwright called for Eleanor a few days later, at a time they had previously agreed upon. He was nervous, for their first meeting was still fresh in his mind. But he could see her efforts to make amends for her actions, and that impressed him. He felt that as long as Miss Eves was willing to be friendly, he should be as well.

As he drew up to the front entrance of the house, Eleanor stepped out of the hall clad in a dark green dress and a black velvet cloak. Albert stayed in the carriage as a footman handed her in, then shut the door firmly behind her. Alarmed, Albert said, "Is not your brother accompanying us? Or your father?"

Eleanor looked at him curiously. "No," she said. "Did you think one of them would be joining us?"

Albert's face twisted into a frown. "Well, I had supposed you would have a chaperon to accompany you."

"Oh!" Eleanor laughed, her cheeks slightly pink. "I am a confirmed old maid, Mr. Cartwright. I have not traveled with a chaperon in many years, and do not plan to begin again now."

"I see."

An awkward silence filled the carriage as it started forward, and they swayed and jostled with its rhythm. Albert shifted uncomfortably in his seat.

"Forgive me, Miss Eves," he said at length, "I hope I did not embarrass you."

She smiled. "On the contrary, Mr. Cartwright. Your assumption that I was still young enough to need a chaperon is flattery indeed. It will certainly give Nathan a good chuckle."

"Yes, I imagine it will. Your brother has an excellent sense of humor."

Albert smiled softly, and Eleanor noticed that the expression did not contort his features as drastically as it sometimes did. He noticed her watching him, and the smile on his face faded.

"I owe you an apology, Mr. Cartwright," she said quietly, looking down at her hands, "for my reaction to you the first time we met, in the woods."

He was silent, and Eleanor could see him pull his feet closer together. She cleared her throat and continued.

"I was startled, and your appearance was so unexpected, your features so... surprising, that I forgot my manners in the moment. I hope you will forgive me."

"Do not trouble yourself over it, Miss Eves," he said, resting his hands on the top of his cane. "I have received far worse reactions in my lifetime, I can assure you."

Eleanor peeked at his face. He did not look angry, which was a great relief, but he held himself a bit more stiffly than before. She bit her lip, and dared to ask a question.

"How old were you when..." Her voice trailed off, and she shook her head, blushing. "Never mind. Forgive me."

His mouth twitched. "I was seven."

He said nothing more, and Eleanor did not press the matter.

After traveling in silence a few minutes longer, they stopped at a rather large farmhouse on the outskirts of the village. "This is the home of the Kirks," Eleanor said, climbing out of the carriage.

"And are they expecting us?"

"Well, they will be expecting me," she said, with a sideways glance. "The whole town knows I make the rounds this time of year."

"But they do not know that I am accompanying you?"

They arrived on the doorstep before she had a chance to answer. Knocking briskly on the door, it was opened a few moments later by a young lady in a large apron.

"Miss Eves," she said, bobbing a curtsy. "And—oh! Mr.... Mr. Cartwright!" She stared up at him, transfixed. Albert looked away.

Blushing, Eleanor said, "Sara, is Mrs. Kirk at home?"

"Of course, miss," Sara said, tearing her eyes away from Mr. Cartwright. "Please come in."

Eleanor and Albert followed her down a narrow hallway, to a small but comfortable parlor. Announcing their arrival to her mistress, Sara bobbed a curtsy before making a hasty retreat.

Mrs. Kirk was a jolly woman whom Eleanor had known all her life. Everything about her was round: her nose was round, her cheeks were round, even her face and her frame were round. She set down her knitting and stood as Eleanor entered the room.

"My dear Miss Eves!" she cried, hugging the younger woman to her bosom. "Welcome!" She turned to Mr. Cartwright, and raising her eyebrows said, "And Mr. Cartwright! I declare! How do you do?"

"How do you do, Mrs. Kirk," Albert said, bowing stiffly.

"Well, come in, you two, and have a seat. Would you like some tea?"

Albert sat in awkward silence as Eleanor and Mrs. Kirk conversed for the next half hour. Every so often one of them would direct a question at him, but he would answer it as briefly as possible and lapse back into silence. Mrs. Kirk often cast him curious glances, but they were not unkind, and she never alluded to his malformed face. At first, Eleanor felt nervous for Mr. Cartwright, but by the end of the visit she felt very much annoyed.

They said nothing to one another on the short drive to the Whitmans'. Eleanor hoped that Albert was considering what he could do differently—better—on their next visit. But she was not so lucky.

"How do you do, Mrs. Whitman?" Eleanor asked, when the lady of the house came to the door.

"Why—Miss Eves! And Mr. Cartwright!" Her eyes grew round, and she stepped back from the door. "Do come in."

They followed her into the parlor, where she had been sewing. Two of her children were also there, but when they saw Mr. Cartwright, they squealed in fright and ran from the room. Mrs. Whitman laughed nervously.

"My apologies, Mr. Cartwright," she said. "But you know how

children can be."

Albert said nothing.

They took their seats, and Eleanor removed her gloves. "Are the other children at school?" she asked.

"Yes, all but little Johnny—he's sick in bed."

"The poor dear! I hope it is nothing serious."

"Just a bad cold, I think. Mrs. Jones was here earlier."

The mention of the midwife caused both women to glance at Mr. Cartwright, who sat silently in his chair. From the corner of her eye, Eleanor saw a dark-haired little boy creeping through the doorway, but before she could warn Mrs. Whitman, the boy gasped.

"Look at his face!" he cried.

Both women jumped to their feet, and the boy tore down the hallway, shrieking and crying all the way. Mrs. Whitman ran after him, and Eleanor, not knowing what else to do, followed.

When they returned to the parlor some minutes later, having at last calmed the child and tucked him back into bed, Albert got to his feet.

"Forgive me, Mrs. Whitman," he said with a curt bow, "but if your son is indeed ill, perhaps it would be better if we left. I do not wish to overexcite the child."

"Oh, not at all, Mr. Cartwright! Johnny will be fine. He was only troubled by something his brother told him about... well, it is nothing." She flushed. "He was a little scared by your appearance, naturally, but I told him you were a very good, brave man who earned your scars fighting dragons. And that cheered him up considerably. You know how little boys are."

She smiled timidly, and Eleanor glanced at Albert's face. He was as white as a ghost, and his jaw was trembling.

"Thank you, Mrs. Whitman," Eleanor said quickly, "but I believe we must be off. I shall call on you another time."

She hurried out the door after Albert, who had turned on his heel without a word, and soon they were back inside the carriage.

"That did not go as well as I would have liked," she said with a sigh.

"I should never have come," Albert said, glaring out the window.

"I thought you wanted to come!" Eleanor said, her patience wearing thin. "Do you not wish to make a place for yourself here in Littleton?"

"There is no place for me here."

"Well, I don't suppose there could be, with that sort of attitude," she snapped. He looked at her incredulously. "Mrs. Kirk was more than civil—she was kind and attentive, and you did not even return the courtesy! And Mrs. Whitman, the poor woman, was only trying to be helpful. You cannot blame her for the behavior of her children."

"I certainly can," Albert said. "Fighting dragons, indeed!"

"He is a *child!*"

"Children ought to be taught manners."

"Manners rarely come to mind when one is frightened, Mr. Cartwright—surely you must know that."

He looked at her sharply, and she flushed, remembering her earlier confession.

"If Mrs. Whitman had *not* come up with the story about you fighting a dragon, Johnny would have been terrified of you for the rest of his life. Is that what you want? To frighten children?"

"Of course not!"

"Then the least you can do is *attempt* to care about the people we are visiting. Try to forget yourself for ten minutes, Mr. Cartwright—can you manage that?"

Albert knew not whether to be impressed or offended that she was speaking to him thus. Never before had someone been so bold with him. With a jolt, he realized what it meant.

She was no longer afraid of him.

A curious sensation came over him, and Albert wondered at the realization. She was not the first woman to address him without fear or trepidation—that honor belonged to Mrs. Lewis—but she was certainly the first single lady to do so. And one of the first in his class of peers. Knowing that he had, somehow, through his awkward, offended manner, managed to break through her fear far enough that she felt comfortable enough to censure him, was strangely satisfying. Satisfying, and humbling, for she was certainly in the right.

Eleanor was looking out the window in stubborn silence, but she turned when he cleared his throat. "Forgive me, Miss Eves," he said. "I fear I have offended you. And probably Mrs. Kirk and Mrs. Whitman as well."

"Undoubtedly," she sniffed.

He frowned. "I am trying to apologize, Miss Eves—the least you can do is *attempt* to care."

Eleanor's eyebrows shot up, and her mouth dropped open. For two seconds they stared at one another, until she suddenly burst out laughing. His mouth twitched, and soon he was grinning as well. Eleanor held a stitch in her side, wiping tears of mirth from her cheeks.

"Forgive me, Mr. Cartwright," she said, trying to catch her breath. "You are absolutely right. I certainly deserved *that!*"

He chuckled. "I am happy to see that your sense of humor is as well-developed as your brother's."

"Nathan has always been the more jovial between us, but his influence has certainly been felt." Finally in control of herself, she smiled at him. "Friends?" she asked.

"Friends," he said. "And I promise to make a greater effort on our future visits."

Albert was true to his word. When they visited old Miss Anderson a few days later, he kindly inquired after her cat, who was curled up on a threadbare cushion in the corner. This attention endeared him so quickly in her eyes that she could not stop speaking his praises for a fortnight. And at the Symons' home, he sat and listened politely as Mrs. Symons described, in great detail, the new pattern of lace she was knitting. Gradually, Eleanor observed that Albert grew less and less reserved, and more and more attentive. While she had at first been afraid of her neighbors' reactions to him, her heart now swelled with pride after every meeting.

"Come again, Miss Eves," Mrs. Sotherby declared one afternoon, waving to them from the doorway. "And you too, Mr. Cartwright. I'd love to hear more about your travels through Europe."

Eleanor waved in return, grinning at Albert, who limped along beside her towards the carriage. "Well, Mr. Cartwright?" she said, as they settled in for the ride back to Edgewood. "How do you feel towards the people of Littleton now?"

Albert grew thoughtful. "I confess to having had little faith in this experiment at first, but after a week of accompanying you on your rounds, I believe it is starting to work. I never knew how interesting people could be."

Eleanor smiled. "Interesting enough to continue the experiment a little longer?"

He glanced at her face. Eleanor was looking at him with perfect affability—as if she did not even see the scar along his face anymore. A strange feeling passed over him as he watched her, and she raised her brow, waiting for his answer.

"Yes," he said quickly. "As long as you would still like my assistance, I am happy to continue."

Her look softened. "I should be very glad of your company, Mr. Cartwright," she said.

And she meant it.

Chapter 9

Albert Cartwright no longer sat alone in a pew at church. Almost as soon as he began showing up at their homes with Eleanor Eves, the townspeople of Littleton opened their hearts to him. Now, before he could even find a seat, his neighbors were stopping him in the vestibule, greeting him in the aisle, and inviting him to sit with them in their pews. A few of the children and even some of the adults still looked at him with trepidation, but for the most part, they were courteous and kind, and it made Eleanor glad to see it.

Albert, too, was beginning to change. After two weeks' worth of visits, he no longer held himself rigidly and spoke only of the weather. Now he found interest in the people with whom he interacted, and he was surprised to find that they, too, had an interest in him. Not merely morbid curiosity concerning his scars, but a real concern for his person and pursuits. Before long, he was conversing with them with ease, and Eleanor even saw him smiling at them from time to time.

December came to Littleton on a fierce, freezing wind, and the first week of the month was unusually cold. Eleanor, concerned for the welfare of a few families in the parish, raided the linen closet and packed up a few blankets and shawls to take to them. She placed them in the carriage, along with a few canisters of soup, and made her way across town.

She first stopped to see the Medfords. They had five children, and because Mrs. Medford was often ill, they were regularly neglected. Eleanor spent an hour tidying the house, bathing the children, and seeing to their needs. She adored children, and since she had none of her own, she relished the chance to cuddle and care for them. She left the family with some soup and a loaf of crusty bread, and made sure that Mrs. Medford and the baby were tucked in warmly before she left.

From thence, she traveled to the Bryants'. They were an aging couple with no living children, and were thus required to care for their small farm alone. The wind bit through her muffler as she emerged from the carriage outside their home. Pulling her cloak more tightly around her shoulders, she carried her parcels to the front door and knocked. It was immediately opened by a tall gentleman in just his shirtsleeves, whose surprised expression mirrored her own.

"Mr. Cartwright!" Eleanor gasped.

"Miss Eves! Do come in—it is frightfully cold outside today."

Dazed, Eleanor stepped into the small front room. What was Mr. Cartwright doing here? And in *such* a state! Eleanor looked sideways at the man standing beside her. His hair was disheveled and his cravat untied. She blushed, and averted her eyes. What was going on?

"Miss Eves! Land sakes, but you're here! At last!"

"How do you do, Mrs. Bryant?" Eleanor said with some confusion. "Have you been expecting me?"

"Land sakes, my dear, of course! When it got so chill last night and the door was nearly froze shut, I said to Jebediah, I said, 'Jeb, mark my words, Miss Eves'll be here in the morning, bringing us some soup and some cheer, I have no doubt.' That's what I said, I did. And here you are!"

Pleased, Eleanor smiled. "I am glad that you feel you could count on me. And you are right—I have some soup for you, and some blankets. Have you been warm enough?"

"Land sakes, no. We run out of firewood the night before last, and what with Jeb's lumbago, we had no way of getting any. But Mr. Cartwright came to call this morning, and he was good enough to go out and cut a cord for us from the grove out back."

Eleanor raised her eyebrows at Albert, who had retied his cravat and was shrugging into his jacket. He caught her eye and offered a small smile.

"That was very good of him," Eleanor said, turning back to Mrs. Bryant.

"Indeed it was. I don't know what we'd have done if he hadn't stopped by!"

A dozen questions tumbled about in Eleanor's mind, not the least of which was how Albert had managed to cut a cord of wood with his lame leg, but she forced them away in order to concentrate on the task at hand. She unpacked the blankets she had brought and wrapped one around Mrs. Bryant's shoulders.

Placing the soup to warm on the stove, she sliced a loaf of bread and set it out with a crock of butter. Albert stumped into the bedroom to check on Mr. Bryant, who was resting, and came back supporting the elder man on his arm, while he leaned upon his cane.

"My, that food smells good," Mr. Bryant remarked, coming to the table. "Would you care to sit down with us?"

Eleanor waited for Albert's refusal, but instead he smiled. "Thank you, Mr. Bryant. It would be an honor to dine with you and your wife."

Eleanor was flabbergasted. Could this be the same Mr. Cartwright who, only a month earlier, had hidden his face from the world, determined to live in solitude? She would never have dreamed that he would willingly dine with a family such as the Bryants, but as they sat around the table, her disbelief turned to amazement.

Far from wanting to hide his face, Albert met the gaze of everyone at the table. His inquiries after Mr. and Mrs. Bryant were obviously sincere, and she saw with great joy that neither of them seemed at all repulsed by his appearance. She watched their exchanges with wonder, marveling at the change in her neighbor.

When it was time to leave, Eleanor promised to check in on the Bryants in a few days, and to send Nathaniel over to chop more wood. "There'll be no need of that," Mrs. Bryant beamed, "for Mr. Cartwright has already made arrangements for us until Jebediah can get up and around. Land sakes, he's such a wonderful man! I declare, Mr. Cartwright, I never had any idea of your being so kind. I certainly hope you decide to settle in the neighborhood for good."

Albert laughed to hide his embarrassment. "It is my pleasure, Mrs. Bryant. I fear that my neighborly concern is dreadfully overdue, but I am happy to be of service to you now."

Albert and Eleanor left the house together. Eleanor, too amazed to think of anything to say, walked in silence beside him until they reached her carriage.

"Mr. Cartwright," she then said, looking up at him. "I cannot tell you how pleased I am to hear of your willingness to help the Bryants." Looking down, she added, "I confess that I was very much surprised to see you here, but I am happy to hear of your genuine concern for their welfare."

"You give me too much credit, Miss Eves," Albert said with a slight shake of his head. "I have been terribly remiss in my duties towards those in our neighborhood less fortunate than myself. You have opened my eyes to the position I have long neglected: that of friend, neighbor, and benefactor. And for that, I thank you."

An odd feeling settled in Eleanor's stomach as she studied his face. Underneath the scar, it really was a handsome one. And though his countenance was grave, his eyes were alight with his newfound purpose.

"You are very welcome, Mr. Cartwright," she said warmly, extending her hand.

Surprise flashed across his face, but he took it, raising it briefly to his lips before letting go. He then helped her into the carriage, and with a slight bow, bid her good day.

Chapter 10

Eleanor had planned to go with Mrs. Lewis to collect the last of the donations the following week, and then finish pricing and sorting the new contributions. Considering the tediousness of the latter task, and the time-consuming nature of the former, she decided to enlist the help of her brother and their neighbor. A message was dispatched to Cartwright Manor; her invitation accepted; and at two o'clock in the afternoon, she found herself seated across from Albert Cartwright in the drawing room.

"I did not get the chance to tell you before, Miss Eves, but your drawing room looks marvelous," Albert said, admiring the new brocade curtains and the lush, patterned carpet.

"Thank you. I am very pleased with how it has turned out," Eleanor replied. "We have only to hang a few more paintings, and then it will be complete."

"It is a very nice room. You have done yourself great credit."

"Don't tell her that, Cartwright," Nathaniel groaned from his place near the fire. "It may go to her head, and heaven knows what she will get into her mind to refurnish next."

They laughed, and Albert inquired after the preparations for the bazaar.

"Everything is going splendidly," Eleanor said, clasping her hands. "In fact, that is what I called you here to discuss, Mr. Cartwright. I have need of your assistance again. And my brother's."

"I am at your disposal, Miss Eves. What would you have me do?"

"I have a list of items which various families in the community have pledged to contribute. Some of them lie quite outside the boundaries of town, and it will take a great deal of time to visit them all and collect their donations."

"And you would like us to collect them for you?"

"Yes, if you would, please. That will leave Mrs. Lewis and me free to finish the other preparations for the bazaar."

"Consider it done," Albert said with a smile.

"Do I not even have a say in the matter?" Nathaniel asked, arching his brow.

Eleanor laughed. "Of course not! You are my younger brother, after all. You are duty-bound to do exactly as I wish."

The following Tuesday was decided upon as the day in which Albert and Nathaniel would gather the donations. Eleanor gave them a list of where they were to go and what they were to collect, and the gentlemen put their heads together to figure out the best route to take between the houses.

"After the Symons, let us call upon the Lloyds," Albert said, consulting the paper between them. "That will give us a chance to stop and check on the Bryants. And then we should visit the Murdochs."

Nathaniel gave him a curious look. "Since when do you know the names of all the families in town?"

Albert laughed self-consciously. "Since your sister helped me see what a decent neighbor looks like."

Eleanor smiled to herself. The Albert Cartwright currently sitting in her drawing room, discussing the needs of the parish with her brother, was certainly not the man she had run into in the woods two months ago. She shook her head in wonder.

The rest of the week passed in a blur. On Tuesday, Nathaniel rode over to Cartwright Manor, and the gentlemen went to gather supplies. When they returned at the end of the day, Eleanor had cleared a large space in the parlor for the new acquisitions.

As the servants began carrying in the donations from the carriage, Albert stepped into the room. Glancing around at the boxes and piles already there, he let out a low whistle.

"Are you not afraid of being lost amid the chaos?"

Eleanor smiled. "Wait until you see the actual bazaar. We shall have more jams, tarts, and pies than you could eat in a fortnight."

He raised an eyebrow at her. "Do you know how much I can eat?" She laughed, and his smile grew broader. "Would you like some help?" he asked.

"If you are offering, I will gladly accept. Mrs. Lewis was helping me earlier, but she had to return home, and I would like to take care of the things you and Nathan have just brought in."

She then explained to Albert how she was organizing the donations. Directing him to a pile of blankets, she asked him to sort them by size.

"How long have you been running the bazaar?" Albert asked, holding up a small quilt.

"Nearly six years."

"And before that, you tried to fill the needs of the parish alone?"

"Not alone, no. The townspeople helped their neighbors when they could—Littleton is full of good, generous souls! And the minister and his wife helped, of course. But even between us, we could only do so much. My father suggested I start a campaign, and the idea for the bazaar was born." She smiled, her voice taking on a hint of pride. "It is now twice as large as it was when I began."

"I can well believe it! And all of these donations are from within the neighborhood?"

"Yes. My father is very generous himself; he always ends up ordering 'too many' of various items in the months leading up to the bazaar. Of course, the 'extras' end up as donations."

"What about this furniture?" Albert asked, indicating an assortment of chairs and a sofa pushed up against the far wall.

"Yes, those are donations as well. We did not replace all of the furniture in our drawing room, but we did replace some of it. Naturally, we wished to pass along the items we no longer need. They still have a great deal of wear to them."

"You have furniture, clothing, linens, household goods, food— what can I possibly contribute?"

"Pardon?"

Albert's look softened. "You have canvassed the neighborhood thoroughly in search of donations, but you have never yet come to call at Cartwright Manor to ask for *my* pledge. What do you still have need of?"

Eleanor looked around sheepishly. "We have so much already, Mr. Cartwright. It is not necessary for you to contribute anything."

Albert was not satisfied. He took a step towards her and looked earnestly into her face. "Please, Miss Eves," he said, his voice low. "What can I do?"

For a moment, Eleanor could not breathe. He was too close, and his manner too familiar. The look in his eyes was so warm that she blushed to think it was directed at her.

She stepped away. "I suppose…" she began, trying to collect her thoughts. "If there was anything I wished we had more of, it would be fabric, so that the families can make the articles they need."

"Consider it done," Albert declared. "I shall be glad to purchase several bolts of fabric and have them sent to Edgewood directly."

"Thank you, Mr. Cartwright. That is very generous of you."

"Think nothing of it," he said. He bid her good day and departed, leaving Eleanor to wonder why her stomach had felt so strange when he looked at her.

Mr. Cartwright did not stop at the fabric. When he overheard Eleanor wishing she had some poultry to distribute, a dozen chickens showed up at her door, packed in a large crate and squawking to high heaven. When Nathaniel let slip that his sister was worried about having enough tables to display everything, a servant from Cartwright Manor arrived to let her know that several tables would be at her disposal on the day of the event.

The community gathered together the second weekend in December to decorate the church. Garlands of pine boughs, tied with crimson ribbon, were waiting to be hung from the rafters. Several men climbed up the ladders to attach them to the walls and ceiling, while the womenfolk wove the branches together below them.

Eleanor was working side by side with Mrs. Lewis in the church vestibule, forming the fragrant boughs into wreaths.

"Mr. Cartwright seems to be far more comfortable with everyone," the older woman said, nodding through the open door in his direction. Albert was standing in the middle of the chapel, leaning upon his cane, trying to find something to do. Eleanor smiled.

"Yes, he does. And what a change has come over him! I almost do not recognize him."

"Oh?" Mrs. Lewis said with a sly smile. Eleanor laughed.

"I see your look, Mrs. Lewis, and can hear your voice in my mind. But do not speak it—do not even think it! Mr. Cartwright is a confirmed bachelor, and I am quite satisfied with my current lot in life."

"I shall have you know I was thinking nothing of the sort," Mrs. Lewis said, arching her brow and trying not to smile.

"Oh, well…" Eleanor stammered. She reached for another branch to hide her flushed cheeks.

"Thank you for allowing him to help with the bazaar," Mrs. Lewis said.

"Thank you for suggesting it. I confess that I was shocked when you did so—I knew not what to think! But it appears that *you* knew what you were about, and it was exactly what Mr. Cartwright seems to have needed."

"I believe the whole town needed it," Mrs. Lewis said gravely. "I shall never forget how distracted and appalled everyone was, that first Sunday he turned up at church." She shook her head.

Eleanor tied a large bow to the bottom of her wreath and held it up, admiring it.

"Miss Eves?"

The women looked up to see Albert Cartwright standing in the doorway. Eleanor colored. How much had he heard?

"Yes?" Eleanor replied, flustered.

"I feel so useless out there. I cannot climb a ladder, and it would feel awkward to help the ladies... have you any job for me to do?"

"You could always play with the children," Mrs. Lewis suggested.

Albert blanched, and the three of them turned to look in the main hall. Several young children were running around, sneaking cloves off the oranges and playing tag between the pews. As they watched, a few turned to look at Mr. Cartwright, whispering amongst themselves before tossing him a smile and scampering off. Slowly Albert shook his head.

"I... do not think I am ready for that," he said.

"Which is perfectly fine," Eleanor said quickly. "We are nearly done with the wreaths, or I would invite you to help us tie the ribbons."

"We *are* done," Mrs. Lewis said. "I am finishing the last one now, and then we shall have enough to hang on each of the windows."

Eleanor looked down, busying herself with the bow on her wreath, but she could feel Albert's eyes on her face. She colored. Why was he watching her? What did he see?

"Miss Eves, I am going to take these out," Mrs. Lewis said, adding her wreath to the pile on the table.

"Let me help," Eleanor quickly replied.

"I believe I can manage," Mrs. Lewis said. Then, with a rather impish smile she added, "Besides, you look as though you are having a bit of trouble with that bow."

Eleanor dropped her eyes, the color rising in her cheeks even as her friend sailed away. After a moment, Albert cleared his throat.

"Miss Eves," he said, his voice subdued. "I would like to thank you for allowing me to help with the bazaar." He smiled crookedly, the scar pulling on his lower lip. "Although it is now plain to see that you really did not need my help at all."

"Oh, how can you say such a thing, Mr. Cartwright! You have been a very great help to me, and I am so glad that Mrs. Lewis suggested it."

"We make quite a good team, I think," he said.

"Y-yes, we do," Eleanor replied, looking down once more.

The silence stretched between them as Eleanor fussed with the ribbon. She glanced up, and found his face only inches from her own. His eyes were warm and inviting, and she realized for the first time what a lovely shade of blue they were.

"Miss Eves," Albert said quietly. "Do you think–"

"Nora!"

They both turned to see Nathaniel striding towards them, his arms full of branches. "Where would you like the rest of these?"

"Oh—just set them over there, please."

He put them where she indicated, and Albert moved away. "I will check on things in the chapel," he said, turning on his heel and limping away.

"Nora? Are you all right?"

Eleanor's gaze shifted from Albert's retreating figure to her brother, standing on the far side of the room. He had pine needles stuck in his hair, and she let out a shaky laugh.

"Of course! But you ought to look in the glass. We could tie a bow about your neck and hang *you* for a decoration."

He laughed and headed off, leaving Eleanor alone to wonder what Mr. Cartwright had been about to say.

Chapter 11

The week before Christmas finally came. The bazaar was scheduled for Friday, and on Monday, Eleanor commissioned her brother, Albert, and all the gentlemen whose help they had secured, to remove the pews from within the chapel. Father Lewis stood by with only a slightly concerned look upon his face. In the three years he had been minister of the parish, nothing untoward had happened during the bazaar, but it still made him nervous to see his sanctuary turned topsy-turvy for a week.

When all the pews were out of the way, Eleanor directed the tables to be brought in and set up. Several carts were waiting outside, filled to overflowing with donated items. Later in the week, the women of the parish would bring in their baked goods as well, filling the chapel with the delicious aromas of puddings, breads, pies, and tarts.

It took most of the afternoon to get everything settled, and when at last they shut up the church the weather had turned. The clouds were thick and gray, and an icy wind was blowing. Eleanor looked up at the sky with concern.

"I do hope we will not have a storm on the day of the bazaar," she said to Albert, who was helping her to the carriage.

"What is a little snow? Nothing the neighborhood has not seen before."

"Yes, but some of the outlying families may not wish to travel through a snowstorm," she persisted. "You know how unpredictable the weather can be this time of year."

"My dear Miss Eves, do not worry yourself so! Let the weather take care of itself—you cannot change it, so do not let it trouble you."

"You are right, of course," she sighed, settling herself into the carriage as he followed after her. "But I would be so disappointed if anything should prevent the bazaar from going forth."

"Nothing to do but wait and see," Nathaniel said, pulling the carriage door shut after climbing in himself.

Though it was only four in the afternoon, it was nearly as dark as night by the time they reached Edgewood Park. Eleanor wrung her hands the whole way home, worrying one of the little pearl buttons at her wrist so much that it fell off. She sighed, tucking it into her reticule so as to prevent its getting lost.

As Eleanor stepped out of the carriage, a blast of wind tore at her bonnet, pulling on the pins and mussing her hair. "Oh!" she cried, clutching at it. "Nathan, do hurry! I think we have arrived just in time."

"I have been feeling it in my leg all day," Albert said gravely. "This might be a bad one."

Eleanor hurried inside, hoping he was wrong. But to her dismay, the wind continued to increase, the temperature dropped, and snow began to fall before they had retired to their beds. By morning, it had not stopped. In fact, with the coming day the storm grew worse, and the wind whipped the icy flakes about so much that nothing could be seen from the windows but swirls of white. The groomsmen had to tie a rope from the back entrance of the house to the stables, to prevent themselves from getting lost in the storm.

Eleanor paced and fretted, both hands on her stomach. "There is nothing to be done about it, Nora," her brother reminded her. "You may as well settle in to play cards with us, rather than stare out the window all day."

"Nathan is right, my dear," Mr. Eves said. "Come, sit with us."

But Eleanor could not settle down. The longer the storm raged, the more uneasy she felt. Near dinnertime, a terrific crash brought her running down the stairs, to find that a tree on the south lawn had fallen, and one of the branches had broken through a window in the drawing room.

The glass was swept up, the branch cut and hauled away, and the open window boarded up, but Eleanor was shaken. What further damage would occur before the storm was spent? Were her friends and neighbors well? Could the bazaar continue as planned? A knot formed in the pit of her stomach as she thought of the poor families who would not be served a Christmas dinner this year, if the bazaar was canceled.

Oh, when would this wretched snow ever cease!

The household went to bed on Tuesday night while the storm was still raging, but sometime in the night, the wind blew itself out. Snow was still falling from the sky when morning came, but it was thin and feather-soft, without a single puff of wind to blow it off its downward course.

Eleanor looked out the window into the park and gasped, as much in delight as in dismay. The entire world had been transformed into a glittering, white, fairyland—perfect and pristine. Gently sloping mounds marked the places where bushes and shrubs stood, and many of the trees were buried up to their branches. The land was a colorless canvas; even the horizon could not be seen, for the pearly sky blended seamlessly into the milky white landscape.

The first order of business was to dig themselves out of the house. Nathaniel and a team of servants began the task before breakfast, but it was well past dinnertime before they had finished. The wind had drifted the snow into mounds as high as a horse in some places, and whisked away the powder until it was barely a dusting over the dirt in others. At last there were paths cleared to the stables, the carriage house, the steward's cottage, and down the lane, but when Eleanor inquired after the state of the main road, her brother just shook his head.

"There is no going out in this, Nora," he said. "Not unless you want to disappear."

More than the one tree on the south lawn had fallen. All over the property, trees and branches, some as thick as a man's leg, were broken and down. The devastation was more than Eleanor had ever seen before, and her concern for the rest of the neighborhood grew.

Late in the afternoon, Eleanor observed from the window a horse and rider, struggling through the snow towards the house. She did not have to wonder who it was, for his appearance came as no surprise.

"Are you all well?" Albert asked, the moment he entered the house.

Eleanor smiled weakly. "Yes, thank you."

"I observed a tree down upon the house, has there been any damage?"

"Only to a window in the drawing room."

"I am sorry to hear it. Trees are down on my property as well."

"Do you think…" Eleanor began, but then she shook her head. If Nathaniel said the roads were impassable, there must be no going through them. Albert guessed her question and smiled sadly.

"I am sure you are anxious to get into town and see how your friends have managed," he said. "But there is no possibility of a carriage getting through."

Eleanor sighed, defeated.

"Give it a few days. A horse and rider can pass through as needed, and once the road has been broken a bit, you may be able to get a carriage through."

It was Friday before enough of the snow had been tamped down or melted to make an excursion to town possible. Albert called on Eleanor shortly after breakfast, his carriage ready.

"I have plenty of blankets and hot bricks inside," he said.

"And I was able to make it here with only minimal trouble. Would you like to attempt a trip into town?"

"Yes, please. I am most anxious to see how the others have fared."

"Then let us go."

It took them twice as long as usual to make the four-mile journey into Littleton. The road was rough, and on two separate occasions the carriage became stuck. Albert was obliged to get out and help his driver dig the wheels free. Eleanor watched through the window as Albert, his balance thrown off by his lame leg, struggled to shovel out and tamp down the snow around the wheels. At last they turned onto the main road in town, and Eleanor breathed a sigh of relief, glad they had finally arrived.

The little church where Father Lewis preached was perched at the end of the street, across from the general store. A large oak tree grew right beside the building, older even than the town itself. It had withstood many storms in the course of its life, but it had at last succumbed to the wind and snow.

The carriage stopped in the middle of the road in front of the church, and Albert and Eleanor climbed out. Eleanor stared, dumbstruck, at the mass of branches poking out from above the church walls. Where the roof should have been, the massive tree now lay, its spindly limbs reaching out of the crevice like an animal trying to claw its way out of a cage. The small apartment adjacent to the chapel where the Lewises lived was completely crushed.

"The Lewises," she breathed.

"Hallo, there!" Albert called, dropping his cane and stumbling through the snow towards the broken building. Branches and debris were scattered all around, half buried in the massive drifts. He clawed his way to the door and began pulling and prying at the splintered wood, attempting to get in.

"Mr. Cartwright!"

Eleanor's head whipped around at the sound of Father Lewis's voice. A sob of relief caught in her throat when she saw him hailing her from across the street, his wife huddled beside him. Grabbing her skirts, Eleanor ran towards them, scrambling through the thick, white powder.

"Oh, thank goodness you are all right!" she said, falling upon her friend.

"Yes, we are well, though quite shaken."

"What happened?" Albert asked, coming up beside them. He was breathing heavily from the exertion of trying to get into the church, and he clutched his leg.

"Mr. Cartwright, you are hurt!" Eleanor cried.

"Never mind that now," he said, his brow furrowed. "I shall be all right."

"We were dining at the Mathesons' when the storm hit on Monday," Father Lewis said. "We felt sure we could make it home before the snow, but they pressed us to stay. It is a mercy that we did, for it meant we were not inside when the building was struck. We arrived in town last night to find it thus."

Eleanor was shaking as she looked back at the church. Twigs and branches reached through the jagged shards of glass at the windows, and half of the front wall had crumpled beneath the weight of the massive trunk. She could not see how anything inside would be salvageable, and tears sprang to her eyes as she thought of all that had been lost.

"We have been staying with the Granthams, above the store," Mrs. Lewis said.

"That is very kind of them," Eleanor said, drying her eyes. "But you must come and stay with us at Edgewood until we can get the chapel rebuilt. We have far more room than the Granthams, especially with their children and the store to manage."

"But that might not be until spring!" her friend protested.

"Then you shall stay until spring," Eleanor asserted.

"I do not know how we shall make the repairs…" Father Lewis murmured, looking at what remained of his church.

"Leave that to me," Albert said. "I have far more time and means at my disposal than you have at present. We shall sort it out."

Eleanor joined the coach driver, who was scouring the snow around the carriage for Albert's walking stick. At last it was located, and she handed it to Albert, who smiled his thanks and sighed, leaning upon it.

Eleanor returned his smile. How glad she was that he was here! If she had come into town and discovered this horrific sight on her own, she knew not what she would have done. Suddenly he looked down at her, a startled expression on his face.

"What about the bazaar?"

Eleanor had been trying not to think of it, but at the mention of the bazaar, she choked on a sob. "Oh, Mr. Cartwright!" she said, burying her face in her hands.

"There, there, my dear," Mrs. Lewis said, rubbing her shoulders. "All is not lost! Perhaps there might still be a way to hold the bazaar."

"No," Eleanor said, wiping her tears, "there is no way to go forward with it now. Besides, it is of little consequence, considering that now the parish has not even a chapel wherein we can gather together to worship."

Albert withdrew his handkerchief and handed it to Eleanor, who accepted it gratefully. Mrs. Lewis continued to comfort her friend.

Frowning, Albert turned back towards the crumpled building. The wind had picked up, blowing cotton-like puffs of snow along the road. "Come," he said, indicating the carriage behind them. "Let us get everyone back to Edgewood, where it is warm and safe. We can decide on a course of action to take from there."

Despite Eleanor's protests, Albert insisted on returning to the chapel the next day and seeing what of the donations might be salvaged. Nathaniel went with him, and they were gone for the better part of the day. Eleanor paced and worried, constantly looking to the sky outside the windows, lest another storm strike while they were so vulnerable.

"Mr. Cartwright seems intent on securing your good graces," Mrs. Lewis observed, as Eleanor once more went to the window.

"He is merely concerned about recovering the goods the town sacrificed so much to provide," Eleanor responded, not looking at her.

Her friend laughed. "I have seen the way he looks at you, my dear; in church, and in town. Dare I suggest that Mr. Cartwright is beginning to fall in love with you?"

"With me?" Eleanor repeated, coloring. "No, Mrs. Lewis, you must be mistaken. Mr. Cartwright cannot possibly be falling in love with me."

"Oh? And why not?"

"Because I am so old!" Eleanor laughed, her blush deepening. "I am most certainly a confirmed spinster, and I told Mr. Cartwright so myself on one of our earliest outings."

"You are still quite young, Miss Eves," her friend said gently, "and who is to say that Mr. Cartwright would not like a more mature wife? There is certainly nothing in his looks or manner towards yourself which suggests that he finds you ineligible."

"That may be," Eleanor said, twisting her hands together, "but I am sure you are wrong."

She sat down on the chaise and picked up her embroidery. Mrs. Lewis smiled gently, but did not press the matter further, for which Eleanor was glad. She absently made a few stitches. What Mrs. Lewis said had crossed her mind as well, but the idea of Albert Cartwright being in love with her was perfectly absurd— nearly as absurd as the thought that *she* might be falling in love with *him*.

Chapter 12

Albert and Nathaniel returned with more than Eleanor thought possible. They had gone on horseback, and taken two other mounts to load with any supplies they could salvage. Both horses were piled high with blankets and clothing, and a few baskets filled with various other articles.

"However did you manage to get all this?" Eleanor asked, as they were unloading the horses.

"Nathaniel found a way into the building," Albert said. "From there, we dug our way through the snow and around the tree. Some of the tables were smashed to pieces or lying underneath the trunk. But several had hardly been touched; we were able to retrieve a good deal more than we anticipated."

He turned to Mrs. Lewis, who was sorting what they brought into piles. "We tried to get into your home," he said. "But there was no way in. I am sorry."

"Do not trouble yourself so, Mr. Cartwright," she said, smiling warmly. "There was not much there that cannot easily be replaced."

The little village was heartbroken to discover that the church had been destroyed, along with the Lewises' home. Friends and neighbors plowed through the snow to Edgewood, to talk over the storm and offer their help and assistance to the Lewises.

"There is nothing like a tragedy to bring a community together," Father Lewis remarked, after another set of visitors had taken their leave.

"That is true," his wife said. "But we are not the only ones who were affected by the storm. Several others received damage to their homes and farms as well."

"Yes, and many of them were not very well-off to begin with."

"That reminds me," Albert said, turning to Eleanor. "What do you plan to do with the items from the bazaar?"

"I have been thinking of that," Eleanor said. "There is no way to go forward with the bazaar now, but you and my brother were able to save so many of the contributions, why can we not donate the items you salvaged directly to the families in need?"

"An excellent idea!" Mrs. Lewis cried, clasping her hands together. "And I can help Mrs. Jensen bake up some things for us to take as well."

"Wonderful!" Eleanor said. "Let us make the deliveries on Christmas Day."

Mrs. Lewis took herself off to the kitchens to discuss the plan with the cook, and Albert smiled. "I knew you would find a way to help more than just the Lewises," he said.

She blushed. " 'Tis the season for giving, is it not? Besides,"

86

she said, her eyes sparkling, "what else am I to do with all those chickens you sent over?"

Eleanor and Mrs. Lewis put their heads together and determined the three families in Littleton who were most in need. They then took inventory of all that remained of the donations.

"There will be plenty to go around," Mrs. Lewis said with satisfaction. "And that is not considering the poultry and the baked goods we shall also be able to contribute."

"I only wish we had some toys for the children," Eleanor sighed.

"Perhaps you should ask Mr. Cartwright," Mrs. Lewis said, her eyes twinkling. "I am positively sure he is a magician, for he has been able to produce everything you have asked of him."

"He is a good man," Eleanor said with feeling. "I wish there was something I could do for him, to show him my gratitude for all he has done."

"Perhaps all the gratitude he needs," Mrs. Lewis said, turning away, "is a little encouragement."

"Mrs. Lewis!"

The older woman laughed. "Forgive me, my dear, for being so frank. I am only thinking of your happiness."

"And you believe my happiness depends upon Mr. Cartwright?" Eleanor sniffed.

"Not entirely," Mrs. Lewis said with a coy smile, "for it also depends a great deal upon *you*."

Mrs. Lewis excused herself to find her husband, leaving

Eleanor alone with her thoughts. She sighed. The thought of risking her heart—to Albert Cartwright, of all men!—sent her nerves into a frenzy. And yet, deep in her soul, she could not deny the longing for a family of her own. She knew that her chances of marrying anyone now were practically impossible, but if Albert Cartwright was indeed interested in gaining her favor, would she—*could* she—accept him?

Chapter 13

A week after the storm had struck, Edgewood Park was a flurry of excitement. Christmas was but two days away, and the entire household was thrumming with excitement. Eleanor and Mrs. Lewis were busily preparing the bundles of donations they would be distributing. They counted and sorted, comparing the items they had to the needs of each family. Albert stumped back and forth between the rooms, helping with whatever the ladies needed. Nathaniel sat in a corner of the parlor and grinned.

When the final preparations had been made, and Mrs. Lewis retired to her room to rest, Albert rested his cane against a chair and bent down to retrieve a large wooden box. He carried it awkwardly across the room to Eleanor, who was watching him curiously.

"What is this?" Eleanor asked, taking it from him.

Albert grinned sheepishly. "Nathaniel told me that he

overheard you and Mrs. Lewis talking of toys for the children. It is not much, but I asked my housekeeper to dig through the attic at the manor, and she unearthed a small collection of toys from my youth."

Speechless, Eleanor picked up one of the packages that lay inside the box. It was wrapped in plain brown paper and tied with a bit of string. Tears sprang to her eyes as she gently set it back down. "Thank you," she whispered.

"I only wish there was more I could do."

She shook her head, dislodging a tear which streaked down her face. She brushed at it hastily. "You have done so much already, Mr. Cartwright. More than anyone else."

Eleanor placed the gifts in the pile of goods destined for the Fairchilds. They had several young children, and she knew the toys would be treasured.

"Would you like to accompany us to deliver them on Thursday?"

"I would be delighted."

"The Lewises will visit the Worthingtons, and Nathaniel and my father will see to the Smiths," she said, suddenly nervous. "Would you be willing to escort me to the Fairchilds'? That way you can give the children their gifts yourself," she added quickly.

Albert's look softened. "I would like that arrangement very much."

The day before Christmas dawned as bright as a summer's day. The sunlight glinted off the snow like a million tiny diamonds, winking and flashing under the brilliant blue sky. It was warmer, too, and the melting snow settled into haphazard puddles like broken bits of sky.

All morning long, Eleanor hummed carols to herself as she swept throughout the house. Nathaniel came inside carrying an armful of spruce branches and deposited them in the entrance hall.

"You certainly seem in a good mood today," he remarked, as Eleanor took some branches to decorate the parlor.

"Of course I am," she said, making her way down the hall. "Tomorrow is Christmas!"

"Eleanor," her brother asked, his tone casual. "May I ask you a question?"

"Yes?" She stopped and looked back at him.

"Would you mind very much if I invited Mr. Cartwright to join us for Christmas dinner? He is our neighbor, after all, and it would be a shame for him to spend the holiday alone."

Eleanor blushed. "I would not mind, Nathan. But there is no need for you to invite him."

"Oh?"

"No," she said, turning away again, "for I have already invited him myself."

In the evening, everyone gathered together to trim the large pine tree that had been brought in and set up in the parlor. Father Lewis and Mr. Eves discussed the plans which Mr. Cartwright had proposed for building a new church in the spring, while Eleanor and Mrs. Lewis threaded dried berries onto skeins of finely spun yarn. Nathaniel took the strung berries and draped them over the branches, singing Christmas carols with gusto. The ladies laughed and teased him, and constantly asked him to rearrange the decorations they placed upon the tree.

Just as they were lighting the candles on the branches, the housekeeper announced that Mr. Albert Cartwright had arrived.

"I hope I am not intruding?" he said, entering the room.

"Cartwright!" Nathaniel called. "Thank heavens you are come. Now perhaps my sister and Mrs. Lewis will have someone else to torment."

Amid the laughs and protestations this response received, Eleanor glanced at Albert. He was dressed in a dark blue waistcoat, which accented his eyes quite nicely. She thought he looked exceptionally well.

"I am happy to be of use to the ladies," he said, smiling at Eleanor, "if it means that I can stay and enjoy the evening with all of you. The manor is exceedingly lonely and dull at present, and seeing the brightly lit windows of Edgewood through the trees was more than I could bear. I simply had to come and make myself a nuisance."

"You are very welcome to stay, Mr. Cartwright," Mr. Eves declared. "What sort of neighbors would we be to leave you alone on Christmas Eve?"

Once the tree was trimmed, they went in to supper in the beautifully decorated dining room. Eleanor had hung sprigs of holly throughout the house and over the table. Large crimson ribbons hung across the ceiling like streamers, and garlands of spruce boughs gave the room the fragrance of a forest.

"Oh, look! Miss Eves and Mr. Cartwright are under the mistletoe!" Mrs. Lewis cried from the hallway.

Startled, Eleanor looked up. She and Albert, who was

escorting her into the dining hall, had paused just inside the doorway, waiting for the others. Sure enough, a small cluster of waxen berries nestled among dark green leaves hung from the lintel. But what was it doing there? She had specifically chosen *not* to decorate with the indigenous plant this year, though she was not averse to it in general. Usually she hung some over the main entryway, but owing to the prevailing traditions regarding the winter berries, and the sly assumptions of her friend Mrs. Lewis, *and* the fact that Mr. Cartwright was frequently a guest in their home now, she deliberately chose *not* to hang any because she did not want to be caught in an awkward situation.

Such as this.

She blushed, and amid the laughter and cries of her friends and family, she glanced at her brother. He was grinning like a child caught with his hand in the pudding pot.

Furious and embarrassed, Eleanor looked up at Albert. His face was flushed as well, but there was a brightness in his eyes she could not misunderstand.

"Go on, Cartwright, give my sister a kiss!" Nathaniel cried.

"It is bad luck to refuse a kiss under the mistletoe, you know," Mr. Eves called out to his daughter.

"It is not that I wish to refuse," Eleanor said, her face crimson, "but perhaps Mr. Cartwright does not care to participate in such a silly tradition."

Albert looked down at Eleanor, his eyes warm and inviting. "I do not think it a silly tradition. But I have no intention of forcing you to comply," he murmured.

Eleanor pressed a hand to her stomach. "I do not mind," she said, her voice faint. "It… it is good luck, after all."

He raised one eyebrow. "For luck, then?"

Eleanor swallowed. "For luck."

Closing her eyes, she lifted her face, and Albert brushed his lips against hers. A cheer went up from the others, and Eleanor stepped quickly away, pink but smiling. Her lips tingled where they had touched Albert's, and she felt as though she had swallowed a bird, which was fluttering madly around inside of her. She glanced up at Albert, whose eyes were shining, and he escorted her to her seat.

"Thank you," she said, sitting down.

"My pleasure," he replied. Then, lowering his voice, he added. "And thank you for the luck."

Chapter 14

Christmas day dawned as bright and beautiful as the one before. *Happy Christmas!* was on everyone's lips, and Eleanor planted a kiss on her father's cheek as soon as she entered the breakfast room.

"Happy Christmas, Papa!" she said.

"And a Happy Christmas to you, my dear," he replied, squeezing her hand.

The Lewises received her good wishes as well, and returned them likewise.

"When shall we be delivering the bundles?" Nathaniel asked, taking a bite of his breakfast.

"As soon as we have dined. I want the families to be able to enjoy their gifts all day today," she said.

After breakfast, the group gathered in the entrance hall to wait for the carriages. The Lewises would be taking the Eves's carriage, and Eleanor's father and brother would be taking one of Albert's. Eleanor fidgeted with the ribbons on her bonnet, glancing down the lane every few moments.

"Stand under the mistletoe—that may get Cartwright here sooner," Nathaniel called, winking at his sister.

Eleanor glared at him, but Nathaniel only laughed.

Soon Albert's carriages could be seen coming down the lane towards the house. Each carriage was drawn by four large horses, their harnesses covered in bells, which rang out merrily in the crisp morning air. The first carriage came to a stop at the bottom of the steps. Albert opened the door and climbed out, a smile stretched across his scarred face.

"A very Happy Christmas to you all," he said, beaming. The others called out their greetings, and Albert climbed the steps to Eleanor's side.

"Happy Christmas, Miss Eves," he said with a bow.

"Happy Christmas, Mr. Cartwright," she replied, dropping her eyes.

She felt suddenly shy around him, and knew not what else to say. The kiss under the mistletoe had changed everything—how was she to interact with him now?

The others were talking gaily amongst themselves, and soon the servants had finished loading everything into the carriages.

The Lewises were the first to leave. Eleanor waved goodbye as Albert helped her into the second carriage. The housekeeper tucked a couple hot bricks wrapped in flannel around her feet, and Albert laid a heavy blanket over her lap. Once everything was ready, Albert climbed inside, the door was shut, and they were off.

Though Eleanor had known this time was coming—had arranged it herself, even—she found that now it had arrived, she had no idea what to say. How on earth was she supposed to encourage him? Eleanor had not the slightest idea how to encourage a man, especially one she had never thought she would ever *wish* to encourage.

They traveled in silence for a time, and Eleanor took the opportunity to study him. How strange that she was once so repulsed by his appearance! Though the angry pink skin still puckered into folds along his face, his eyes were so kind, and his smile so sincere; she hardly noticed his scar anymore.

He looked over at her, and their eyes met. Tentatively, Eleanor reached a gloved hand out and gently touched the edge of the scar on his cheek. Albert closed his eyes.

"There was an accident with our carriage," he said after a moment, opening his eyes. "The horses bolted when one of them became frightened, and the driver could not control them. He was thrown from his seat and killed. My mother died as well. I was not so lucky."

He sighed, and Eleanor withdrew her hand. "I was thrown through one of the carriage windows as it tumbled off the road. My head and face were cut by the glass, and my leg was crushed by its weight. The doctor thought he would have to amputate, but having lost so much blood from my head wounds, he did not want to risk the procedure."

Eleanor had her hand to her mouth, the image of a small boy, crushed and bleeding, haunting her mind. She closed her eyes. "I am so sorry."

"I have learned to accept what happened. My father went mad

with grief over the loss of my mother, and he directed the anger he felt towards God and man, at me. For years I thought it was something *I* had done to upset him. But it was my disfigurement, not my person, that enraged him. It was a constant reminder of what he had lost, and for that reason he could not bear the sight of me. When I finally realized the truth, I determined to leave as soon as I could."

"When you came of age," Eleanor said, nodding. "I remember when you left."

"Yes." He cocked his head, a curious smile pulling on his mouth. Eleanor blushed.

"What is it?" she asked.

"I have never felt this way before," he said in wonder. "I thought I would feel resentful, letting someone into my heart, but instead I feel relieved." He gripped the top of his cane. "For years, I have felt alone in the world. I never let anyone in because I feared that their reaction to my scars would turn them against me, like it had my father. But this experiment of Mrs. Lewis' has proven otherwise."

He shifted in his seat. "I did not think that anyone would be willing to look beyond my physical appearance; to judge me for who I am, not what I look like." He smiled. "I have never been more happy to be wrong."

"I am glad to hear it," Eleanor said with a smile. "And I am glad that Mrs. Lewis proposed we work together on the bazaar. I might not have come to know you otherwise."

"That would have been a very great pity, for your friendship— and that of your father and brother—have meant more to me than you can ever know. Your family has shown me what it means to love another person. Your care and concern for one another, for me, and for the people of Littleton, has shown me what family really is, and what community feels like."

"And what does it feel like, Mr. Cartwright?"

"It feels like I have a place in the world. There is a sense of belonging that I have never known before. It feels like…" He frowned, trying to find the words. Suddenly his eyes grew bright. "For the first time in my life, it feels like *home*."

He looked as though he wished to say more, but the carriage lurched to a stop, and the moment was broken. Albert opened the door and climbed down the steps, then turned back, offering his hand. The warmer days and freezing nights had left patches of ice everywhere, and Eleanor took it gratefully, not wanting to slip.

A rush of excitement ran through her as she looked up at the Fairchilds' home. A wiry column of smoke twisted snakelike from the chimney, slowly disappearing into the still morning air. Icicles hung from the eaves, and a crude wooden shovel leaned against the house near the front door. Eleanor grinned.

"Shall we?" she asked.

She hoisted a basket of food onto her hip, and Albert tucked the crate of wrapped toys under one arm, leaving him free to lean on his walking stick with the other. The coach driver and footman each grabbed a bundle and followed after them as they made their way up the walk. Eleanor stood trembling beside Albert, who raised his arm and knocked firmly on the front door. It was opened a moment later by Mr. Fairchild.

"Happy Christmas, Mr. Fairchild!" Eleanor cried.

Mr. Fairchild stared at them, dumbstruck. But one of his children, spying the wrapped packages in Albert's arms, squealed in delight and threw open the door. Soon a whooping, giggling, writhing mass of arms and legs accosted Albert, who laughed and relinquished the crate.

"Don't let them stand out there freezin' to death," Mrs. Fairchild's tired voice called out. "Come in, come in!"

Mr. Fairchild stepped back, allowing Eleanor and Albert, followed by the servants, to file into the tiny front room. His eyes grew round at all the parcels they carried, and his wife broke down into sobs.

"Oh, bless you, Miss Eves, bless you! There's not a scrap of food in the house, and I was just tellin' Roger I didn't know what we'd be fixin' the little ones to eat."

"Hush, Mrs. Fairchild, do not carry on so! There is plenty of food here now."

"Aye, and blankets," Mr. Fairchild remarked, unwrapping one of the parcels.

"We knew it would be a difficult season for you, what with the storm we had, and canceling the bazaar..." Eleanor swallowed past the lump in her throat. "But we've brought you a bit of Christmas cheer, and–"

"And toys!" one of the little boys yelled.

There was a general scrambling and shrieking as the little ones tore open the gifts that Albert had brought. Mrs. Fairchild, sitting on the threadbare sofa with a baby in her arms, wiped her eyes.

"Toys! Upon my word! Bless you! Bless you!" she said through her tears.

"Mr. Cartwright made this possible," Eleanor said, smiling up at him. "He and my brother rescued what they could from the wreckage of the church. And the toys are entirely his doing."

Albert modestly ducked his head. "Miss Eves exaggerates. She is the one who organized the entire effort—it is she who deserves the credit."

They laughed, and Eleanor, after confirming that all the packages had been brought in from the carriage, embraced Mrs. Fairchild.

"Please, send me word if you are ever in need," she whispered, hugging the woman to her.

"I will, my dear, I will. Oh, bless you!"

Albert and Eleanor squeezed through the children—who were sprawled across the floor playing with their new treasures—and out the front door. They were not two steps down the path, when the door opened behind them and a tow-headed boy barreled out of it.

"Thank you, Mr. Cartwright," he said, throwing his arms around Albert's leg and burying his face in his trousers.

Completely taken aback, Albert patted the lad awkwardly on the shoulder. "Happy Christmas, son," he said.

The boy showed no sign letting go, and Albert looked helplessly at Eleanor for direction. "Give him a hug," she whispered, her eyes shining.

Slowly, Albert crouched down until he was at eye level with the boy. He knelt in the snow, grunting as he leaned upon his bad leg. The child watched him hesitantly, but as soon as Albert opened his arms, the lad flung his arms around his neck. Albert returned his embrace, holding him close.

"Is it really true that you fought a dragon?" the boy whispered. "Johnny Whitman said you did."

Albert pulled away so he could look directly into his eyes. The little boy did not flinch, but waited eagerly for his answer.

"No," Albert said at length, and the boy's shoulder's sagged. Then, with a twinkle in his eye, he added, "I fought *two*."

Chapter 15

Christmas dinner was a gay affair. Eleanor felt as though her heart would burst with happiness as she looked around the table. The Lewises, displaced though they were, had settled in nicely at Edgewood Park. They were beaming at one another and all those around them. Her father sat at the head of the table, preening like a peacock on display—he loved having a houseful of guests—and Eleanor smiled affectionately at him. Nathaniel sat beside her, deep in conversation with Albert Cartwright, who was stationed directly across from her, and whose eyes occasionally met her own. She blushed to see how warmly he looked at her, and she could not hide the smile it brought to her face.

After dinner, as the ladies excused themselves, Nathaniel leaned over and whispered in her ear.

"What is going on between you and Albert Cartwright?"

Eleanor colored. "Nathan, please! Lower your voice."

He grinned. "I knew it."

"Oh, hush. You do not know anything."

She stood and left the table with Mrs. Lewis, whose arm she took as they made their way into the drawing room.

"What a lovely day it has been!" Mrs. Lewis sighed, settling herself on the settee.

"I quite agree," Eleanor replied, picking up her sewing.

"I am very sorry that after all your work, the bazaar had to be canceled. But I am so glad we were still able to help a few families in need."

"I am glad as well. When I thought of our friends who would be going without on Christmas day—oh! My heart! But it has all turned out quite splendidly."

"You and Mr. Cartwright seem to have sorted things out between yourselves, as well," Mrs. Lewis said, taking up her knitting with a smile.

Eleanor laughed. "Dear Mrs. Lewis! I believe that you and my brother must be working together on some scheme, for you are both intent on seeing what is not there."

"Are you telling me that there is nothing between the two of you?"

There seems to be a great deal between us, Eleanor thought. Instead, she lifted her chin and tried not to smile. "If there is," she said, "it will be for Mr. Cartwright to decide."

They passed a pleasant half hour talking over the day, and the joy that was shared with the families they visited. When the gentlemen at last joined them, Eleanor caught Nathaniel's smirk, and wondered what he meant by it.

The party gathered around the pianoforte and sang carols

while Eleanor played. Mrs. Lewis was prevailed upon to play a few Christmas hymns for their entertainment as well, but only agreed on the condition that she did not sing. As she took her seat at the instrument, Eleanor slipped out of the room. When she returned a short time later, Nathaniel gave her a quizzical look, but she merely shook her head and refused to say anything.

The evening passed as most pleasant evenings do. They talked, they laughed, they made merry, and soon it was time to bid goodnight to their guest. Mrs. Lewis excused herself and retired to her room, and Mr. Lewis soon after joined her. Nathaniel sat playing a game of chess with his father, so it was left to Eleanor to see Mr. Cartwright out.

"Happy Christmas, Cartwright," Nathaniel called, winking at him.

Albert chuckled. "Happy Christmas, Eves. Mr. Eves."

Eleanor was trembling as she walked with Albert down the hall. Would he speak tonight? Was she a fool for hoping he would? He stopped in the center of the entrance hall and collected his gloves and hat from the table there, but Eleanor drifted closer to the door.

"Miss Eves, it has been a most delightful day," he said, bowing to her.

"I quite agree with you, Mr. Cartwright," she said, offering him her hand.

He brushed a kiss on the back of it, but did not let go. Eleanor drew a deep breath, striving to calm the fluttering in her breast.

Albert stood with his head still bent, his focus fixed upon her hand in his. Slowly he traced a circle with his thumb along the back of her hand.

"Miss Eves," he said, finally looking up.

"Yes, Mr. Cartwright?"

"I wonder if…" He hesitated, and his eyes clouded. Looking away, he released her hand. After a moment he turned back, searching her face. Whatever he saw there must have encouraged him, for he smiled.

"With your father's permission," he said slowly, his eyes locked on hers, "I wonder if I might call on you sometime."

Eleanor exhaled, and a slow smile spread across her face. "I would like that very much, Mr. Cartwright," she said.

It was as if he were seeing the sun for the first time. Albert's entire countenance brightened, and he stared at her, unable to say a word. Slowly Eleanor lifted her eyes and fixed them on a point some distance over their heads. After a moment, Albert's gaze followed hers, and a nervous laugh broke through his lips.

"Is that… mistletoe?"

Eleanor dropped her eyes, coloring. "Nathan must have put it there as well."

He cocked an eyebrow at her, and she smiled demurely.

"It *is* bad luck for a lady to refuse a kiss under the mistletoe," she said.

"Well, we do not want that." He cupped her face in his hand, running his thumb along her chin. She closed her eyes, trembling beneath his touch.

And then he kissed her.

Eleanor leaned into him, fire spreading throughout her limbs. His lips, hesitant at first, grew more confident, and he wrapped his arms around her, pulling her close. He kissed her until she felt dizzy, and when he at last drew back, she took a shaky breath.

"That kiss is certain to bring us luck," she said faintly.

"I believe it already has," he said.

"Does this mean you will be staying in Norfolk?"

"Would that please you?"

"Very much."

"Then I shall stay."

She smiled, and, stretching up onto her toes, she kissed him again.

Acknowledgments

I am continually in awe over the abundance of blessings the Lord pours out upon me. I will be forever thankful to Him for His infinite love, His matchless power, and the creativity with which He blesses me, every day of my life.

For my wonderful husband, John. Thank you for loving me, encouraging me, and always being my biggest fan. I love you more than I could ever express.

For Carrie, Erin, and Sachiko, whose help and feedback made this story more amazing than I could have ever done on my own. You guys are a blessing in my life, and I love you!

About the Author

 Shaela Kay was born and raised near Seattle, Washington. She studied Theatre and English at Brigham Young University-Idaho, but left her studies in order to be a wife and a mother. When she isn't writing, you can find her quilting, crafting, or homeschooling her four children. She and her husband John live with their family in a little house along the banks of the mighty Columbia River. Visit her online at www.shaelakay.com.